Cat's CLAUS

Dale Mayer

CAT'S CLAUS: BROKEN PROTOCOLS 4
Beverly Dale Mayer
Valley Publishing Ltd.

ISBN-13: 978-1-773363-87-5
Print Edition

About This Book

Charming Marvin is always thinking, always talking, always learning, always looking for interesting new distractions. After the talking, mega-intelligence enhanced feline inquires when Christmas Day would be in their new timeframe, it sets in motion events that might not make everyone so holly or jolly.

Charming's mistress, Lani Blackburn, realizes that although she's gained so much, she's also lost some things she loved in being brought forward two hundred years in the future by her husband Liev's slightly abnormal, genius brother Milo.

All holidays were banned from society by the government long ago. Though he hates to deny his beloved anything, Liev has no idea what Christmas is until he does a little research that makes him wonder if they can find a way to return the festive miracle to their small family, if nowhere else.

The best of intentions for a wondrous celebration of peace on Earth and goodwill toward mankind quickly becomes very complicated in world that doesn't always know the sentiment, let alone the Christmas spirit…

Books in This Series:

Cat's Meow

Cat's Pajamas

Cat's Cradle

Cat's Claus

Broken Protocols 1-4

Sign up to be notified of all Dale's releases here!

https://geni.us/DaleNews

Protocol 4:6:12. You will in no way use our history to recreate that which we know to be detrimental to our society—particularly if those actions are to selfishly enhance your own authority, position, status, and/or wealth.

Chapter 1

"WHEN IS CHRISTMAS?" Charming asked.

Lani Blackburn looked at her beloved orange Persian cat and grinned. It was a little hard to have any respect for his vast intelligence when he was upside down, four paws to the wind, and twisted in a bizarre curl.

"Remember? They don't do any of those old holidays anymore."

"So? That's them. Then there's us." He snorted out a sneeze and flopped over on one side. "And the two don't have to be the same."

Sometimes the darnedest things came out of that cat's mouth. And where was this all coming from? "Are you missing the holidays?" She quirked her lips and laughed. "You hated the noise, the company. Really howled when I sang Christmas carols."

"Ha!" He rolled over to glare at her. "Anyone would howl at your singing."

While she was still gasping at his barb, he continued, "I liked the tree. It was fun. Adored the tinsel." He grinned evilly. "Loved the cookies."

She remembered the last Christmas in Technicolor

memories. Charming climbing up the pathetic fake tree, until it collapsed on top of him. The problem of him constantly trying to eat the tinsel and her finding the tinsel and plastic needles everywhere, but the cookies? … She groaned out loud. "You used to take a bite out of every one."

"I had to see which one I wanted," he said in such a reasonable tone of voice that she had to laugh.

"Christmas tree? Tinsel?" Liev, Lani's husband, who was technically a couple hundred years younger than her, sat down on her chair with her. She grinned, as the furniture stretched and sprawled to accommodate the extra person. That never got old. Her *husband*—and what a trip that still was to say or to contemplate—held a mug of something hot.

"Is that coffee?" she asked accusingly. "And you didn't bring me one?"

He leaned over and kissed her. "I brought enough to share."

"*Blech*." Charming rolled over in such a way that his butt was presented.

"Charming, don't you fire that thing," Liev warned.

But gentle snores were already working up and out of her beloved dust ball of a cat.

"Christmas," she murmured, images of past holidays floating through her head. She didn't even know what time of year it was right now. They were currently on a Pacific island paradise. After all the hell they'd been through getting here, she'd wanted nothing more than to crash in peace and to recuperate after her time-traveling side effects—something that was taking longer than expected.

Her body still hadn't fully adjusted to her new surroundings or the atmosphere a couple centuries in the future. Neither had Charming's. And their original trip here to this time era hadn't exactly been a fun one—or one she'd agreed to. But Milo, Liev's genius kid brother, had devised a computer program that had snatched her from the twenty-first century and dumped her here two hundred or so years later, practically in Liev's arms as a gift for him. Thank goodness she'd been holding Charming at the time. Milo had added enhancements for her to better adjust to her new life, only he hadn't known to adjust his calculations for Charming. As a result, Charming had been given enhanced communication skills.

Lani wished she'd have gotten something because not only could Charming talk but he was a wizard when it came to the latest technology.

He matched Milo perfectly.

Affectionately Lani glanced at Milo. His massive mohawk was orange now. She couldn't help but wonder if it wasn't to show his solidarity with Charming. She wouldn't put it past him.

Both Liev and Milo had decent relationships with their family, but it was distant. Then again, that might have been because of genius Milo's work. The security around the two men was something else. Milo had a seriously scary brain. When he'd created the time-travel program that had hauled her out of her life, he'd created a hell of a mess.

Now he was working on something else. Genius was to be allowed at all times, as Milo had created some amazing inventions, but genius also needed to be watched. Up until now, Liev kept tabs on his brother, like a hen trying to keep track of twenty chicks. It worked but not well.

"What are you doing, Milo?"

"Research."

"Of course," she said patiently. "Research on what?"

She tugged Liev's mug toward her and took a sip. The one thing they did wonderfully well in this century was coffee. Lord, it was good. Travel was another one. Planes had been relegated to the annals of history, as the dirigibles had been in her time. Now they could punch in a code and walk through a portal. She loved that.

And she'd quickly fallen in love with her new husband. Their relationship was in its early stages for them though. A honeymoon phase, so to speak. Still, as honeymoons went, it was pretty great, once they'd gotten over the attacks, attempted kidnappings, and murders that had arisen after her time-travel event.

She smiled.

"What's that look for?" Liev glanced at her, his eyes warming.

"You. Us." She loved that about him. He hadn't had much long-term relationship experience before she'd landed almost literally in his lap, but he'd blossomed since.

So had she. She felt blessed to have him in her life.

Maybe the other two felt the same as well. The four of them made up their family unit. She knew a few people she might one day learn to call friends, but, because of the many pitfalls in this new life waiting to trip her up, she was hesitant to get cozy with anyone. After all, the conversations were limited to keep her past a secret. Then again, she'd also gained some notoriety recently, and many people had heard of her by now.

How weird was that?

Cool too. She'd been transformed from a number in a city of big numbers to someone special here.

She'd still rather trade it all in for the ability to navigate the minefields that awaited her. She didn't understand the most basic things here.

"Christmas."

Milo's distracted voice pulled her from her musings. "Christmas?" She shook her head. "You don't do any holidays anymore, do you?"

"No. Too many protests from dissident groups all the time. As the protests became more violent, we had to ban more and more of them. Now they don't exist."

Holidays gave people something to look forward to, something to celebrate. Who in a normal workforce didn't love the thought of getting an extra day off because the holidays were coming? And the thought of family and friends gathering for Thanksgiving and

Christmas—two of the biggest holidays in her time—made her reminisce about the past.

It was sad in a way. No special neighborhood gatherings or celebrations had happened since she'd arrived here. Families apparently tried to get together on a regular basis, but she could easily see how that would go by the wayside very quickly as everyone's lives ramped up.

The thought of missing Christmas put Lani in a melancholy mood.

She had great memories. Even alone with Charming, they'd had fun. She'd put treats on top of the tree, and he would climb up the needle-covered branches time and time again. Sometimes it worked well and sometimes not so well. she'd laughed a lot, sometimes cried, but they'd had each other. Lani had had Christmas parties at work too. Yeah, those memories brought a wince to her face, but at least they'd been memorable.

"What was Christmas all about?" Liev asked, his tone curious.

"Togetherness," she said instantly. "Family. Friends. Rejoicing in the experience of being alive and sharing what you had with others."

She smiled reassuringly at him. Okay, so it was a little smile, but her lips did twitch, so it counted. Liev worried about her. Always. He was wonderfully considerate. And she loved every minute of it.

A huge diesel engine kicked in. She glanced over to find Charming grinning at her upside down. She reached for him and rubbed his tummy. "You loved the turkey dinners."

"And the gravy."

She didn't think it was possible, but Charming's grin widened. Then his eyes turned huge. "Is it lunchtime? Did I miss lunch?" He rolled over and snapped to his feet. His gaze locked onto poor Liev, and, if Charming could have mentally forced Liev to get up and feed him, he would have.

A side effect of the time travel.

Her appetite was not as ravenous as Charming's, but now that Charming had brought up food, her stomach growled in sympathy. Charming turned to look her way, and his grin widened. He knew Liev might ignore her cat's demands for food, but he'd never ignore Lani's.

"Fine, food it is then."

"Thanks, Liev." She accepted the still half-full mug of coffee from him and sat back. Another great thing about her relationship was that Liev loved to cook. In a world of automatic food, it was his hobby. He cooked the same way people in her time did. Not her, of course. She'd had a penchant for fast food and pizza, whereas Milo had a preference for those disgusting health shakes.

She shuddered just thinking about them. She and Charming had been forced to drink them in the beginning to help them recover. Not fun.

But now, with Liev looking after them as well as he

did, she knew they'd both landed on their feet in a clover patch.

Life was good.

LIEV WANDERED INTO the kitchen to sort out a meal for everyone. *Everyone* being the four of them. Milo might join them, but he ate like a bird. Charming, on the other hand, ate like a tiger. So odd.

Still, Liev hummed in the space he'd had renovated to suit his needs, which essentially mimicked his kitchen at home, and pulled out the makings for big thick sandwiches on fresh bread. As he cut the bread, his mind drifted to the Christmas issue. Not only did his century have no religious or fun holiday traditions, like Lani had grown up with, but no celebrations to look forward to either, like she'd also mentioned. He vaguely remembered seeing something about the holidays in his history lessons. That had been a long time ago. He'd most likely downloaded them and assimilated the information into his brain without considering the significance of it. As it had no relevance to his life at the time, he had stuffed it back into his deepest memories. Now, he not only wished he'd paid more attention but he wondered just what he'd missed out on himself.

His childhood hadn't been lonely per se, but it hadn't been overwhelming with love and fun either.

He'd taken over Milo's care at an early age after their parents' death. That had taken all the fun out of his life. Milo even seemed to have stopped his mental development at the age of sixteen. And that took a lot of patience. With Lani joining their tiny family unit, Milo had mellowed out and had fallen into line in many ways, accepting the feminine rules without argument. Lani even convinced him to join them for meals, so they could have family time.

Liev hadn't really understood what that meant, but he cherished the time she'd carved out for the four of them. Yes, he included Charming in that group. Good luck keeping him out. They did have to work on his manners though. Lani tried, but, any time she got distracted, Charming would sneak food off her plate and scarf it down before she had a chance to stop him. Even when Liev doubled the cat's portions, Charming would still pull the same tricks.

As a result, Liev had dialed down the portions—much to Charming's disgust. Even now, Liev could feel those huge golden orbs locked on his every movement as he made lunch. He had made an egg salad yesterday, which remained in the fridge. It was an old-fashioned recipe with pickles in it. He'd had to scrounge those from a specialty shop, and it had cost a fortune.

At least he had one of those.

And as long as Milo continued to devise the wild and wonderful things he invented, that wouldn't change anytime soon.

"Lani, Liev is daydreaming again," Charming tattled.

Liev shook his head at Charming's not-so-subtle way of saying Liev was slow to bring the food to the table. Lani might be working on the cat's manners, but a lot of improvement was left to be had. Liev grinned.

He and Milo had both lived a bachelor lifestyle, and, wow, had that changed.

In a good way—at least for Liev. He glanced at his kid brother to see him muttering like crazy over his screen.

Liev frowned when he realized that the screen on this side of the monitor had been blacked out, so no one could see what Milo was doing. Studying his genius brother's features, Liev figured Milo was just deep into his research and turned back to making lunch. Bringing out a fresh pineapple that he'd paid an exorbitant price for, Liev quickly prepped it and portioned it out.

"Lani said she'd trade her egg salad for my pineapple," Charming piped up with a hopeful look.

Liev shook his head. "I wasn't giving you pineapple to begin with."

"Then I'd better be getting more than my fair share of egg salad," he groused.

Liev grinned like an idiot. How had his staid, stressed-out, overworked life become this combination of a loving, laughing lifestyle instead?

Just lucky, he guessed.

"Milo, come join us. We're sitting down to eat,"

Liev said, as he finished plating the food.

"Be there in a minute."

Liev walked to the table and held the plates up until Lani made it to her seat. Otherwise Charming—precariously balanced on his back legs—would have tried to take the plate with the bigger portions.

When safe, Liev placed the plates down and took his own seat.

Minutes later Milo joined them, one of his nasty all-natural green good-for-you-if-you-can-get-it-down concoctions sitting in front of him.

Liev caught sight of Milo's gaze and followed it back to the opposite side of the table. He stared in horrified fascination as Charming tore into the pile of chopped eggs on his plate. Bits and pieces were spilling off his chin and back onto his plate, much of it falling onto the surrounding table.

Even Lani stared.

Charming finally noticed. He lifted his head, surveyed the mess, rolled his eyes, and tried to clean it up a little. Then, as if realizing he would just make more of a mess soon, he shot them a dirty look and went back to eating the way he'd been before.

"Just one big happy family," Liev murmured.

"And aren't you blessed?" Lani laughed.

"I so am."

Chapter 2

THEY WERE ON vacation, a beautiful isolated spot along the ocean. Liev had told her the location but the geography had all changed now so the name Broger Islet meant nothing to her. The cabin, which had already been remodeled by Liev looked like so much was the same yet was so different.

She loved being near the coast, walking along the beach, swimming in the water. The lack of people. Privacy for the family to sort themselves out as to what the unit would look like long term. She loved it all. Yet even here she had her schooling to do. Even more important now.

Later that afternoon, after a dizzying amount of elementary-level schoolwork to get her acclimated to her new surroundings, Lani's mind once again wandered in the direction of Christmas. It wasn't as if she couldn't do without it, but it would be nice to have a few of the better things from her old life incorporated into her new one. Christmas was one of them. But she didn't need the trappings of the old holiday to make a day to celebrate. She wasn't sure she needed the same date. That was nostalgia talking. They could just pick a day and have it then. Besides, she wasn't sure what day Christmas would equate to today. She supposed the super-duper computers of this twenty-third century could tell her. Hell, those things could tell her what the weather had been in the city she'd been born in on the exact time and date of her birth. Not to mention every other demographic piece of information available.

The Christmas idea percolated in the back of her mind. She wouldn't have to make a big deal out of it. And she wasn't sure Liev or Milo would be on board with such a concept, but Charming would love it. And, since she loved him, maybe, just maybe, she could make it happen for him.

After the others saw how much fun it could be on a small scale, maybe they'd want to do something bigger next year.

She grinned. The issue had been decided. She'd make Charming a Christmas celebration. There may not be the same religious or commercial aspects to it, but one thing would be the same. She, no, *they* all had a lot to be grateful for, and Christmas was a wonderful time to give thanks. Hell, Thanksgiving would be wonderful as well.

She stared out at the lazy sunset as it slowly dropped, her toes curling into the warm sand. She'd lost track of time. The days of the week, the calendar for the months. The years never had clicked for her, and now that she was centuries ahead of her time, she really couldn't get any perspective.

But this was a place to start. Maybe she could do something special for Valentine's Day too. She bet Liev or Milo had never celebrated such a thing in their lives. Well, she could do something. As she glanced at their Pacific beach home, humming with techno geeks inside, she wondered if she could do something in secret. Or did that just mean everyone would know?

And whose help could she employ to make this happen? It was not as if she had friends to enlist, and she didn't dare let Milo in on it. Like any teenager, regardless of his twentysomething status, he couldn't keep a secret. Especially from his brother. As she mulled it over, she wondered if she could somehow pull off a trick and surprise them all.

Her mind turned back to the fancy computer equipment Milo had put together for her to learn about their advanced high-tech lifestyle and newer customs. She found it hard to believe that she still only worked at the elementary-school level, while Charming had pranced in a half-dozen times, listened for one-quarter of the time that she did, and now listened to university-level stuff.

"If I could wish for one Christmas gift, it would be for enhancements of my own, so that I could learn faster and could retain more," she muttered.

"Ha. No Christmas gifts here. Remember?" Charming wandered in front of her and down at the water's edge, where he stared hopefully into the water that teemed with fish.

"You just ate," she said in exasperation. "Besides, the fish know you. They aren't stupid enough to get close again." And know him, they did, but not in the way he might want to remember. He thought of himself as a big bad hunter, but his last attempt had him going for an unexpected swim. She grinned at the memory of the soaked orange ball and Milo's solution to stick him in the upright dryer. Poor Charming. He'd looked like a puffer fish for hours.

Charming, as if understanding what she was thinking, spun and glared at her.

Instantly she wiped the smile off her face and glared back at him.

Injured pride kept his back stiff and his tail upright as he stalked back inside. "Isn't it time for you to get back to primary-school lessons?" he tossed back snidely.

She gasped. "That's just mean."

"Bite me." And he stomped inside.

Maybe she wouldn't make a Christmas celebration for him after all.

Liev hated to leave Lani even for the day, but he'd avoided showing up in the office for too long. He'd have to change that.

He couldn't help but wonder if this was a good time for her to try a few hours on her own. She'd been doing so well. He knew she was frustrated with her slow progress in their education system and her lack of enhancements, but it wasn't exactly something they could order off the shelf. They had to customize it for her.

And that meant it would take a bit of time.

Milo appeared to be in one of his resting phases, as compared to his brilliant driven-to-get-a-concept-from-his-head-into-form phase. Maybe they had all needed a break after the stress of the past few weeks. They'd return home soon, but Liev needed Lani to adjust emotionally and philosophically to her new status. And what a status that had been. From obscure in the shadows to a celebrity of sorts. That phase would calm down, but, every time she opened her mouth to answer questions from her adoring public, she was in danger of blurting out something that would reveal the truth of her background.

The education system they'd dug out of the archives wasn't ideal, but, as it ran independently without connecting to the other computers or the government system, it was perfect for her right now.

Except it was slow.

And they didn't have much time.

CHAPTER 3

LANI RUBBED HER eyes. The stupid computer was giving her a headache after only a couple hours. Why was it so hard to figure out when Christmas—if they still had that particular holiday—would be in today's calendar? She'd been through several databases and had been overwhelmed with links to follow, but the actual term *Christmas* appeared to have been deleted from their history. She'd entered *Easter* and *Thanksgiving* and *Halloween* and got the same response. Outside of a short description of what each of the holidays were historically, no further information existed on the type of celebrations that took place or when it officially happened. She just didn't get that.

Was she the only person left in the world who knew Christmas was December twenty-fifth? Then again, that had been the day for her, but she remembered European consultants who had worked at her old company for a while, and they celebrated an earlier day in December. She found no mention of any of these holidays in the twenty-third-century computer systems. This time period hadn't just made the holidays illegal, they'd wiped them out completely.

She snorted. Sounded like the same thing they'd tried to do to her people. Or rather, the Naturals, the people her name was now associated with. Given that she'd only been trying to do the right thing, it was nice that the association gave her a reasonable cover for her continued ignorance of the way things worked here, as the Naturals were a fringe group who'd lived their lives disconnected from mainstream society.

She was rather hoping to be further along in her adaptation into her new life, but living on a Pacific island didn't give her too many opportunities to learn.

And, with Liev so quickly producing clothes and other necessities while she watched, she wondered if shopping could happen otherwise, like at malls, small boutiques, or even online. He said it did, but he didn't understand why one would bother, when he could just input it in a program, and it would instantly use her form to model each design on the monitor. The ones she liked, he only needed to push a button, and damn if the printer didn't just create it for her. She'd had to stop him at one point. She'd been enthralled and had loved the dresses, the different underwear. He'd been all over those too. But she felt guilty about the added expense. She didn't know how much all that cost, but she could only wear one outfit at a time.

When they had arrived on the island, he'd made a dozen different bikinis, each one getting less and less material, until she was afraid to look at the next one, in case it was a single G-string. But he'd outdone himself on the tropical skirts and sundresses. Even now, she'd only had a chance to wear half of them. She loved it.

But he had the ultimate control on her wardrobe. She didn't. If she were shopping in a store, it would be a different experience. And one she missed. She knew his income was much higher than most other people's in this place, so not everyone would have access to what he did, but she was delighted that he did. She had said she needed a pair of slip-on sandals to walk on the beach, and he'd downloaded a program and let her choose between a half-dozen different designs. Then, when she was just about to make a choice, he decided that she needed to try them on the sand to see which ones she loved and proceeded to create them all.

She glanced at the white stretchy sandals she carried in her fingers. That was the other thing. One size fits all. Like the furniture, when anyone stepped into her sandals, they automatically adjusted to fit the foot. God, she loved this stuff. She'd tried to get Charming to stand in one of her sandals when she'd first gotten them, but he'd been too smart and had given her one of those looks that said, *Do you think I'm stupid?*

Yet all this technology was precisely the problem. How could she even begin to give Liev a gift when not only could he make and buy anything he ever wanted but there was nothing he wanted?

Milo was the exact same. It wasn't like Lani was an artist and could paint him something personally. She could hardly bake them a special dessert, when Liev ruled the kitchen and all the ingredients. She might enlist Charming's help there, as he was known to successfully steal from the kitchen, but she knew that Liev wasn't fooled as to his outgoing inventory. He just let Charming get away with it.

She really wished she had a creative streak. If she could write, she could write a special poem for Liev. It could be intimate and personal.

Lani sighed. There was nothing she could give to these two brothers. They already had everything.

THE WALL HOLO shut down as Liev pinched the bridge of his nose. Maybe he did need to return to the office for a few days. It shouldn't be happening, but it seemed like the place was falling apart on him.

"Trouble?"

Milo stood behind him. Liev turned and gave his brother a reassuring smile. "Not really. I'll just have to show up at the office more often. When the boss is away and all that."

Milo nodded even as he curled his lip. "Figures. At least say hi to Tommy for us while you're there."

"Will do. Reports say he's doing well in the training program. Should be ready to start full time in another month or so. How are you doing on that personal portal device?"

Milo shrugged. "Haven't been working on it."

Liev's eyebrows shot up. "Why not?"

Milo shifted his weight and tucked his hands behind his back. Then he shrugged. "Got sidetracked."

"Damn." Trying to keep Milo on track was a full-time job. He was into the creation process and much less the detailed final stage required to make something user friendly enough that it could be brought to the market. He constantly wanted to leave projects when it hit the tedious stage. The new shiny idea always beckoned him away.

"Christmas," he said in a low tone.

"Say what?" Liev walked closer. "Did you say, *Christmas*?"

"*Ssshh.*" Milo shot him a warning look. "Charming is too damn smart. He'll hear you."

Running a hand through his already-tousled hair, Liev stared at his brother, trying to figure out why Charming would give a damn. "What about Christmas?" he whispered, playing along.

"I was trying to research the holiday. And, like, nothing is there to research. It's not right," he complained. "We should have access to all information. Not just what they want us to know."

"Ah." Now it made sense. Milo, being the brain he was, was offended that some information had been secreted away, so he couldn't learn about it.

Yeah, that wasn't good. Best to nip this in the bud.

"Take it up with Stephen," Liev suggested. "Lani has shaken things up a lot within the Council, but I warn you. I doubt that sufficient change has happened to make enough of a difference yet. Especially with regard to the flow of information—particularly archived information."

Milo looked undecided, then muttered, "I'll think about it." And he walked away.

Liev stared at him in consternation. Milo *thinking* about anything could mean everything, from making the company millions to destroying something major, depending on which side of that decision he landed on.

Just then, Liev's holo beeped, and he had to return to the mess at work.

Now if only Milo would concentrate on *his* work. Life would go so much smoother.

Chapter 4

L ANI WOKE EARLY the next morning, careful to not wake either Liev, who slept soundly at her side, or Charming, who snored on his back—all four paws to the wind—at her feet. It was almost impossible to do anything on the sly in this house. Still, she escaped to the kitchen and brought up the big 3-D counter computer. Entering several commands, she left it humming and went to the coffeemaker, setting it to make a wonderfully rich cup to start the morning.

With cup in hand, she walked back to the computer and studied the information. *Great.* One wasn't allowed to buy real trees in this world now. Didn't that figure? She looked outside at the palm trees just waking up under the bright morning sun and frowned. She was not going to decorate one of those. She would as part of the larger design but not for the actual Christmas tree. She sent out more search requests for fake evergreens. She didn't dare search for Christmas trees. That much she'd learned already about her new home. Not only would it likely trigger alarms somewhere, the search could easily send a trigger email to Milo and Liev. So not what she wanted.

She waited and watched. She'd logged in as *Liev* deliberately, so that no one would know what she was up to.

There.

The screen flashed with several options. Now were any of those good ones? She mulled over the options and prices, saved two to consider later, and carried on searching for lighting. That almost made her give up. What on earth did any of those terms mean? Whatever happened to simple LED lights? Or the colored glass lights, the racing lights? Were they all gone? And, if so, what had they been replaced with?

Frustrated, she closed down that search and tried to find decorations. But that was too broad a search. She needed to narrow it without mentioning *Christmas* or *holidays*. She tried *tree decorations*. Then *ribbon style decorations*. Then *glass balls, painted wooden miniatures*. Too much and too many choices, and yet nothing came with hangers. She frowned, cleared her search pages, and shut it down. Damn it. There had to be an easier way to find stuff.

Even ordering, shipping, and storage had to be dealt with, but she wouldn't have to worry about those if she couldn't find anything. She walked outside with her coffee and considered asking one of her three male family members for help, then immediately tossed the idea. She wasn't ready for her secret to be spoiled yet. Her fighting spirit had been pushed to the forefront now. There had to be something she could do.

As she looked around the bushes and trees, she envisioned lots of little lights, maybe ribbons, maybe little glass balls. Who knew once she got started? She just needed to find the stuff. Or maybe she could make some. She used to make some wonderful origami. She could do a few of those for the tree—but not tons. And it still didn't nullify the need for a special tree and lighting.

"Couldn't sleep?"

Liev sat down on the top of the deck, a mug of coffee in his hands. She sat beside him. "Just a lot on my mind." His searching gaze bore into the side of her cheek. She linked her arm with his and laid her head on his shoulder. "I'm fine."

"Good. I'm glad to hear that." He dropped a kiss on her forehead. "Anything I can help with?"

She shook her head. "I've just got a few things to work through."

He wrapped an arm around her and hugged her. "If you need to talk …"

"I know. It's not major, and it's not serious. I just want to do something and have to figure out how."

His face twisted with effort, and she knew how hard it was for him to hold back. To not push. To not pry. "You did a great job with Milo," she said.

His eyebrows flew up, and he stared at her. "Really? I can't say that I see it myself."

His droll tone made her giggle. "It couldn't have been easy."

"No. Nothing with him is easy. Not even when it's supposed to be."

She laughed. "He's a good soul."

"True enough."

Sitting together in the morning dawn, it was hard to find anything wrong with her world.

"Breakfast? Surely you didn't forget to call me for breakfast." Charming's plaintiff cry wobbled toward them.

Lani turned to see him sitting in the doorway. "Hey, big guy."

His jaw opened into a huge yawn. "Is this what morning looks like?"

She grinned. "Yes. And stop kidding around. You're often up at this hour."

"Only while I'm getting a snack or a drink or something …" He sauntered forward until he reached her. He lifted his nose and smelled the air experimentally. Then he shuddered. "Still smells too fresh. Too real. Too *morningish*."

She stroked his back. "You'll survive."

"Yeah, I will." He dropped to his belly and sprawled sideways across the deck, his head hitting it with a *thud*. "But I won't like it."

She scratched his belly, and damn if a wave of love didn't wash through her. He was so special.

He rolled onto his back and stretched his legs up as far as they'd go and offered more belly.

In silence they sat, enjoying the morning.

Until a roar came from inside.

She winced. Surely it hadn't been her searches earlier on the computer that had brought such a reaction from Milo? *Surely?*

Out of the corner of her eye, she caught Charming's expression before he jumped to his feet and disappeared around the bushes.

Milo came storming out. "Who was on my computer?"

Ah, shit. She immediately apologized. "Me. I'm so sorry. I was just trying to do some research."

Liev tugged her close. "Milo, she has to have access to a computer somewhere. Just because you're here doesn't mean all the computers are yours."

She risked a glance at Milo to see him grabbing his mohawk with both hands and pulling it in frustration. "They don't have to be *all* mine ..."

"Then what's the problem?" Liev asked in a no-nonsense tone.

"*Arrgh.*" Milo spun on his heels and left.

Liev chuckled. "Don't worry about it. He's a little possessive."

"A little?" She worried about what evidence of her activities she'd left behind. She didn't really want them to know what she was doing, but, if Milo wanted to know, he could find out easily enough.

Feeling despondent and not a little crowded by her lack of privacy, she stood and walked down to the water.

"Don't worry about Milo," Liev called to her.

She tried to smile back at him, and, seeing the worry on his face, she knew her smile attempt was a giant failure. "I'm fine. I'm just going for a walk."

She sensed his indecision as she walked away. She wouldn't mind a few minutes alone. She should just ask him for a computer of her own. They probably had dozens in the place back home. The problem was that they were all connected somehow, so, no matter what she did on one, they'd know about it on the others. What she should have done was use her school computer. That wouldn't have brought any raised brows. It was older and only used for training. Meaning it hadn't been used for years before she came around.

Too bad she hadn't thought of that this morning.

Charming raced up behind her and passed her at a steady gallop, his tail flying high. She ran past him and startled him, causing him to book it. Laughing, she gave chase. They ran down the beach until she couldn't run anymore. When they'd first arrived in this world, all kinds of exertion had tired her out. Just walking across Liev's apartment had exhausted her.

Now look.

"We're doing so much better now, Charming."

He grinned up at her, his jowls flapping in the wind as they slowed to a walk. "Much better. I really like it here."

"I do too."

"But I wouldn't mind a weekend at a log cabin with

that whole Christmas look."

"And that's something we could probably arrange quite easily." She amended that. "Maybe."

He brightened, then a bit of worry traveled into his gaze. "Not that I want to be outside in winter or anything. That would be cold, wet, and nasty." He gave a mock shudder.

"Then what's the point?"

"The fire. The log cabin. The looking out the window to see a winter wonderland."

The way he said it almost made her nostalgic. "I can ask Liev. It might be possible."

"Great. Race you back." And he took off.

She watched him go, too tired to give chase. She hadn't realized they'd traveled so far down the beach. If she didn't run back, it would take a good twenty minutes of walking. Oh, well. Maybe the walk would be good for her.

Or it would have been, but she'd really tired herself out on that run.

Damn it. She almost wanted to sit down and wait for Liev to find her. Walking in the sand was especially hard. She trudged forward, feeling her energy drain lower and lower with every step.

Finally she sat down to rest.

LIEV LOOKED UP from his monitor for the twelfth time

in hopes of seeing Lani returning. The island was perfectly safe. He had no worries there. But, with the ease of portal travel, anything could happen.

Charming wandered in and jumped up on the desk.

"Hey, when did you get back?"

"A while ago. Why?"

"Did Lani come back?'

Charming plunked his butt down on Liev's tablet—the only thing on the desk—and stared at him. "I don't know. I ran home, and she was walking behind me." He frowned, the furry ridges above his eyes slashing downward. "Is she not home?"

"I don't think so." Worried, Liev walked outside and stared down the length of the beach. In the distance, he saw her sitting at the edge of the water. His stomach twisting, he started toward her. What was going on? This was a side of Lani he'd never seen before. And he didn't like it. She was always so happy, so balanced. The peacekeeper, when Milo and he went at it. She added calm to the troubled waters and her laughter to long tough days.

He walked steadily toward her, so that she had time to see him coming. If she wanted time alone, he didn't want her to feel like he was intruding. But he didn't want to give her too much alone time either. Normally he and she could talk about anything. And did. They had no secrets. Not with Lani. He loved that about her. She was so honest. So transparent.

So he really wanted to know why she was acting like

this.

It had started after Charming's offhand remark about Christmas. He hoped she wasn't missing her old world. He'd deliberately helped Milo destroy the time-travel program and related equipment that he'd used to bring Lani here. It was too dangerous to have around where someone could steal it and pervert it for horrible purposes. They'd had to destroy it. But it had also made sure that she could never go home. He didn't want her to go home. She was his wife in all ways. But especially in his heart.

As he came closer, she looked up. And smiled. A look that went straight to his heart. She was direct. So honest. No wonder he loved her.

"Hi."

"Hi," he responded in a lighthearted tone, his gaze intent. "How are you?"

"Tired." She laughed. "I raced Charming down the beach, but we went farther than I realized." She motioned to the water, as still as glass in front of them. "I started back but got tired, so I decided to sit a bit and enjoy the view."

He plunked down beside her. "Have to still guard your strength. You're doing so well, but it doesn't seem to take much to remind you that you aren't fully adapted."

"So true."

"Do you want to stay here longer or come back where you can lie down?"

She stared out at the water, then back at the distance she had to go and sighed. "It still looks so far away."

He hopped to his feet and held out a hand. "Come on. Nap time."

Laughing, she got to her feet and grasped his hand.

With a big grin, he swung her up into his arms, and, whistling a light tune, he carried her home.

CHAPTER 5

AFTER A NASTY fortifying shake from Milo, she curled up on the hammock outside and napped. God, what a life. As great as it was, she still needed to find her place in this new life. But, as this last incident showed, whatever she ended up doing couldn't require too much of her, or she'd never recover. And Liev wouldn't allow her to work; she was sure of it. Money wasn't the issue, and, as someone who had worked all her life and had worked hard for every penny, this part was easy to get used to. At the same time, she felt almost useless. Liev looked after her completely.

In this century there was no manual housecleaning anymore. No laundry. No cooking, unless one chose to do it. And dishes were also extraneous. For the first time, she was really free to do whatever she wanted to do.

Lying on the hammock, she pondered life in this new age. She needed a hobby. Or to volunteer somewhere. Maybe she could help Liev or Milo in their company? No, not help Milo. He was way past her ability to be of any help. As for Liev, he had hundreds of employees.

He didn't need another one—especially an un-skilled one.

She needed to find something to fill her day. But maybe not just yet.

This Christmas thing could take enough of her energy. Now if only she could solve it. Given that Liev and Milo were busy working, she slipped into her classroom area and pretended to pick up her headset and get to work on her lessons.

Instead, she started working on her computer, the one Milo had set up for her studies. Idle thoughts at first; then she got serious about shopping. She really wanted this whole Christmas thing to happen. Money wasn't such an issue—she had some that Liev had given her. She didn't want to ask him for more, but honestly these prices didn't make any sense. They seemed outrageous even after she took into account the infla-tion for over two hundred years.

She sighed and wondered what it would cost to do this. Would it be possible to just rent decorations? Could Liev's parents have any stashed away anywhere? No, not likely. Still, maybe the rental suggestion was an option. She quickly searched and found hundreds of rental options.

But nothing even close to what she wanted.

Parties. That's what she wanted! *Party supplies.* At least it would give her a place to start. She started with a wide search, then narrowed it and narrowed it and came to … nothing. Absolutely nothing. Were no parties had here in this time period either?

She looked around and sighed. It was lunchtime, and damn if she wasn't hungry again. She'd join them in the kitchen and ask the brothers how the whole party-rental thing worked.

Unfortunately they just looked at her.

"*Party?*"

The delicate questioning tone of Liev's voice had her stopping to stare at him. "What's wrong with the question?"

Milo's wide foolish grin had her slapping herself up the side of her head. "Oh, my Lord. I don't mean parties like Johan's type of party," she cried out. "I meant like a birthday party. An anniversary party. A graduation party."

They stared at her, glanced at each other, then turned to stare back at her. Liev asked, "Birthday party?"

"Graduation party?" asked Milo, a curious look on his face. He got up from the table and walked over to the nearest computer. She knew within seconds he'd have found out all the information available to be found. "So you weren't raised to celebrate your birthdays?"

They shrugged in unison.

She sighed. "No gifts? Birthday cake? Friends over to have a great time together with? No?" The brothers just sat here and stared at her, like she was talking a different language. As she sat back in shock, she realized she was.

They had no idea what she was talking about.

She opened her mouth to ask another question, when the noise of an alarm filled the air.

LIEV RACED TOWARD his wall holo unit as the alarm continued to resound throughout the small house. He had no idea what was wrong, but his computer system had been compromised.

He reached the main machine to find Milo already working away furiously, his face in grim lines. If there was one thing in this world that petrified Milo, it was that someone would steal his inventions. "Milo, what have we got?"

"So far, not much. Looks like something on one of our computers has triggered a kickback on the government bots."

"*Hmmm.*" That made no sense. "Still, I thought we stopped anything like that from happening with the new patches."

"Should have. But something somehow has raised the alarms."

"Is someone trying to hack in?" Liev had his 3-D screen up and busily searched the red lines that showed where the problem was. "It's coming from Lani's old education system."

Milo snorted. "That makes a stupid kind of sense.

That old unit hasn't been used in decades. It probably shorted out. At minimum, it would be using old codes, and that likely would have triggered all sorts of alarms."

"Time to ditch it then."

"Shouldn't have brought it into service in the first place, but the educational software material was on old tech, so it required old-tech hardware to work." He glanced at Liev. "She should be done with them by now, right?"

Liev frowned. "I'm not sure she is."

"I'm not," Lani said in a dry voice. "I'm about halfway."

Milo stared at her, gave himself a mental shake, then went back to working on the computer. "Half is fine. We might need to download the material and put it on a new medium for you though. I can't have it triggering government security bots."

"No, I suppose not." Lani grimaced.

But Liev caught the wrinkle of embarrassment on her face. He hated that. She'd been through so much and had done so well. How could this possibly be easy on her? "You're doing just fine, you know?"

"Ha. It'll take me months to get up to speed on the useful stuff."

Milo shook his head. "Take your time. This stuff is all about our system and how we function in it, so that should be the priority for you."

Liev was happy to see that Milo's enthusiasm had perked up Lani. Milo being the supergeek, he was used to having much less intelligent people around him. He often got frustrated when they couldn't reach his level of genius with a concept he was working on, so he often worked alone. Then it almost always took a translator to bring it down to the level of the minions in the world. Liev was often that translator. Not the same IQ level as his kid brother, but Liev was no slouch. Still, that awareness of how smart Milo was helped Liev to understand what Lani was going through because Liev had gone through it himself all his life. "Maybe we can find an easier system for her."

Milo nodded absentmindedly. He was already back at work.

Leaving the computer, the breach fixed, and the alarms no longer going off anywhere, Liev walked over and gave Lani a hug.

"Does this mean I can't use that system anymore?" she asked in a low voice.

"It would be better if you didn't."

He wasn't sure from the distant look in her eyes if she was upset that her education would take a temporary hiatus or if something else was going on behind those beautiful eyes. Again, there was a wall, a distance between them, and he hated it. "Lunchtime?" he asked.

"Ha! We didn't even have breakfast," Charming accused. He hopped up on the countertop and glared at Liev. "Did you really think I wouldn't notice?"

"Funny, one of the cans of salmon had been opened and tossed in the recycler earlier," Liev snapped and turned Charming's words back on him. "Did you think I wouldn't notice?"

Charming's flat nose went up into the air. "That was *really* early this morning. It was hardly breakfast."

Milo piped up, "Maybe we should check him for parasites."

Charming howled, "What?"

"Hey, it happens to all of us." Milo barely held his grin back. "Your excessive appetite could be a symptom."

"Excessive? My appetite isn't excessive. I'm a cat. What would you know?" Charming stalked toward Milo, his fur standing out at odd angles. Then his attention was caught by something dashing across the 3-D monitor.

"What the—"

Milo cuffed him lightly, and he shut up. Plunking his butt down on the counter, he watched the screens dance by.

Liev frowned. It was very unusual for Milo to actually hit anyone, softly or not, let alone Charming. But what was even more unusual was for Charming to take it.

Under normal circumstances, Milo would be fending off claws and teeth for that attack. He glanced at Lani to see her reaction, but she was staring down into her empty cup. She hadn't even noticed.

And that was another anomaly.

Worried, he led her over to the big easy chair, waited until she'd curled up, and it had expanded to suit her, and then watched in amazement as it stretched upward, as if to cup her. He'd never seen the chair do that before. Lani was enclosed, curled in a ball, with her head resting on the top, as if this were normal.

And maybe it was. Liev just hadn't seen it happen before.

He took the empty cup from her and walked past the other two, still staring at the monitor, on his way to get her a fresh cup. He nudged Milo and nodded toward Lani.

Milo turned to look. He reared back slightly, frowned, looked at his brother, then back at Lani and the chair. He lifted his shoulders in bewilderment. Charming, never one to miss something going on, studied Lani too. Then, being a cat, he jumped down, raced to Lani, and jumped up on the back of the chair, where he lay down by her head. Instantly his engine kicked in.

Chapter 6

"P ROBLEMS?" CHARMING NUDGED her neck when her hand stopped moving on his back.

"Not really, just ... stymied." She loved that word, and it suited her mood. She wasn't as much frustrated as she didn't know how to move forward. And still keep her surprise a secret. At least not now, she couldn't do this alone. Therefore, she might need someone's help. And how could she do that when she wanted something no one knew about, where the concept was so foreign that she couldn't see how to explain it to anyone other than her family without letting on about her secret history? And that had to be guarded.

So what to do?

Maybe give it up, but that really wasn't what she wanted. They had a calendar here, but it wasn't what she was used to. It was part of her next lesson, and, of course, she'd managed to delay that all over again.

They had so many wondrous things here and, sure, apparently a lot of get-togethers, just not as she knew them. Parties like Johan's had probably been around during her century, but she hadn't participated in the swinging-singles' parties or group sex activities. Those she was certain were part of Johan's *party* definition. Apparently Liev, like any healthy male, had also participated—at least initially. Thankfully he'd decided they weren't for him. But it left her wondering about what she wanted.

If she were to bring it up, she'd be reminded of her weakened state still. And, after this morning, that was still true. But maybe not in a few months from now. She could be fully healed—although portal travel still caused her stomach to revolt. Not as bad as the first couple times but still more than she liked, so traveling wasn't an easy solution. Given the amazing times, she shouldn't complain.

Without realizing it, another heavy sigh escaped.

Charming nudged her hand. "Hey. If you are depressed, the best way to get out of it is to be with your pets. I'm your pet, and I need more attention."

She looked at him, and that same big wave of emotion swept through her. She cuddled him into her arms and hugged him tightly. Outside of his initial yowl, his engine kicked into supertanker mode and rolled through the room. "I'm not depressed. I'm just looking for a way to fit in."

He reared back and gave her a beady look. "I told you to lay off the extra treats, you know? If you'd listened, you'd have no trouble fitting into stuff."

Behind her, she heard Liev's strangled laugh. She shook her head in exasperation. "I am not having trouble fitting into my clothes." She glared at him. "I'm having trouble fitting into this life."

He jumped from her arms to the floor, took a few steps, and launched himself up to the counter. "Whatever. If you do need bigger clothes, Liev can adjust the program, you know. Just saying …"

"Charming, that's not very nice." But damn if her hands didn't slip down to her waist and on to her hips, manually judging if she'd gained any weight. Catching his smirk, she glared at him. "It's all right if *you* are useless. You're just a cat, but, in my old world, I worked every day. I don't know what to do with myself now."

Liev studied her.

She raised both hands in frustration. "I know. I need to heal. I need to fully recover. Otherwise I'm a handicap in the workforce. I guess I was thinking I could do something."

"Then find it and do it." Milo's head had lowered as he studied the bottom portion of his monitor. "That's what I do."

She glared at him. "That's not the same thing."

"Well, it is. Find what you want to do. And do it." He stared at her like she was simple, which—compared to him—she was.

"And how do I find what I want to do?"

That made his eyebrows fly upward. "If you don't know the answer to that, how do you expect anyone else to tell you?" He shook his head. "*Know thyself.* Remember that phrase."

She groaned. "You can be so irritating."

"*Hmmmph.* Just trying to help." He pulled out his weird headset, plugged it in, and tuned her out. She knew the words would be showing up on the screen, going directly from his mind to the computer. The technology fascinated her. She'd been good with computers but not gifted, like so many of her coworkers had been. And they would be completely blown away by Milo's talent if they were here.

She had hoped for a future in computers and had quickly come to realize that the only way for that to happen was to receive enhancements to help jump her education forward, like Charming had gotten. Otherwise, it meant years of study, and, by then, she'd have to catch up again, as the technology here advanced so fast.

Liev walked to her, bent down, and dropped a light kiss on her lips. "If you come up with something, no matter how far-fetched it might sound to you, tell me, and I'll let you know if our world has anything similar."

She brightened. "Thanks. That's a great idea."

He led her back to her old education unit, which now looked like some space-age doorknob. "This is what we've set up for you." He quickly showed her how to use the unit. "Give it a try, and see how you do."

Right. So much for feeling like she had a light at the end of her tunnel. She needed to focus and get out of elementary school. Everything else, even ordering stupid decorations, depended on it.

LIEV STAYED LONG enough to make sure Lani was fine with her new computer setup. She'd really been doing well. Considering she was still having these moments of weakness, something Charming didn't appear to share, it was all good otherwise. Charming ate so much more than she did, so maybe lack of nutrition was the answer. She hated Milo's booster drinks, though they were full of wonderful things for her. But she was a foodie like him, and Liev could understand her not wanting to live on the shakes.

Walking back to the main room, he caught Milo and Charming, their heads bent together, whispering. He frowned. Those two conspirators were bad news when they got together. "What's up?"

Milo looked back at him. "Nothing."

Yeah, right. He groaned silently. Just then his office called, reminding him of all the pressing issues he'd been avoiding while on vacation. Yet that had been part of the deal to coming here. He'd take as much time off as possible but head into the office when it was una- voidable. And today it was unavoidable. After a quick call, he said, "I'm heading to the office for the rest of the day. Looks like I'll have to go for several days in a row to sort out some problems."

Milo gave him his attention. "Bad?

"No, and nothing that affects you. Mostly staffing issues and more government troubles from the new

Council forming."

"If you talk to Stephen, let me know. I've been trying to reach him, and he's not answering my calls."

Liev didn't bother answering. He knew that a lot of people avoided Milo at times. When he wanted something, he could be very bullheaded about getting it. If Stephen had had the time to deal with Milo, Stephen would have responded. But, with the fall of the old Council—thanks to Lani, Milo, Tommy, and Johan—Stephen's life had been overtaken with responsibilities as the new Council was being formed.

Liev wanted Stephen to be part of the new Council, but Liev had no guarantee of that happening yet. If ever. The government system was in flux. It was all good, but, just as a lot of corruption had been in the last government, it was all too possible the same problem would exist within the new one. Liev almost wanted Stephen off the Council so that he'd remain part of the government watchdog unit. Someone had to keep the others honest.

Liev opened the portal and stepped into his office. And damn if people weren't already lined up waiting to speak with him. It would be a long day.

CHAPTER 7

L ANI DID AS many of the learning modules as she could before her head started pounding. She hated to admit it, but Milo's shakes were one of the best answers for that. They tasted disgusting but took the edge off the pain immediately, and, usually within ten minutes, the headaches were gone for good. She walked to the main room to find him and Charming busily working on some kind of joint project. She could hear them muttering something about government regulations and firewalls. She rolled her eyes. Nothing the two of them liked better than hacking into stuff they weren't supposed to hack into.

"Hey, Milo, any chance of a small dose of that headache remedy?"

He glanced up, his gaze unfocused. His eyes cleared, and his head bobbed. "Sure." He headed into the other room, his fluorescent yellow-and-black striped pants hurting her eyes. He looked like a bumblebee. Fashion sure had changed. At least Liev was more conservative, but Milo didn't appear to know the word.

He came back with a huge glass of pink stuff. She groaned. "What part of *small* drink did you not understand?"

"The part that says you are trying to avoid your boosters."

Charming snorted.

She glared at him as she accepted the glass. "That's not fair. If I want the headache to go away, I'll have to drink all this, won't I?"

"Absolutely. Just think. If you'd had this earlier, you wouldn't have a headache now."

Morosely, she stared into the pink depths and wondered why there couldn't be a bright pink pill she could take instead. "Why don't you, with all your brilliance, take this liquid and turn it into a capsule, so people could just swallow it?"

"You *are* going to swallow it." He gave her that *you are a simpleton* look again.

"Yes, but, if all this nutrition was packed into one pill, I could swallow it in one gulp and not have to taste it and suffer. This is painful."

"Hey, I made it cream-soda flavored for you this time."

Oh, no. The last time he'd flavored something, it had tasted like a cross between boogers and bubblegum. She tentatively took a tiny swallow and almost barfed. "This is really disgusting," she gasped.

He shot her a look, then went back to work.

Well, she'd asked for it, and it did work, but damn, she'd hoped for something about one-tenth this size. She pinched her nose and proceeded to guzzle it down.

Out of the corner of her eye, she watched Milo and Charming high five each other, hand to paw. She stopped drinking. "Really? How childish."

On cue, both of them imitated her by pinching their noses and drinking from an imaginary glass.

"Oh, all right." She poured the rest of the drink down her throat, then ran to get water to clear her mouth. "There. I drank it. Okay?"

Both males beamed at her, like she was a star pupil.

"Now that I did that, can you show me how to do something?"

Milo stared at her warily. "What?"

"How do I order a gift for Liev? You don't have stores that I can walk into. I could possibly order from online stores, but everything is in Liev's name. All the accounts bill him, and I don't want to bill him. I want to pay for this myself."

He looked at her curiously. "What do you want to order? And, if it's for Liev, why wouldn't he order it himself? Plus it makes no sense for you to pay for it if it's going to be his." Confusion rippled across Milo's features.

Charming, however, was rolling around on the counter, laughing. He understood because he'd come from her century.

Patiently she said, "I want to give him a *gift*. That means, I want to pay for it and give it to him. It's special, and I don't want him to know about it ahead of time."

"*Special.* What is it?"

She shrugged, embarrassed. Because she had no idea what to give Liev. He was a man of means and yet simple tastes. But she might be able to find him an old-fashioned Christmas cookbook or something. Speaking of which, she didn't think they had physical paper books anymore. At least she hadn't seen any. "Don't you have books anymore?"

He shook his head. "Only in museums. You can get everything in holo or digital, and they don't degrade over time."

"Crap." She had to find another way. "If I wanted to get him a cookbook, where would I find one?"

"A cookbook?" Milo rolled the idea around in his head. "Online."

"But then he'd know I ordered it, right?"

Milo nodded. "And he'd get a notification of where he could pick up his holo and how to store it for easy retrieval."

"And if I want to buy him a real cookbook?"

Milo shook his head. "You can't. You could possibly make one. The printer would do that, but why would you?"

Yeah, why would she? *Because* she was looking for something Liev had never had.

"Where could I find the recipes I want to put into this book to print?"

That earned her another sideways glance. "On the computer."

She sighed. "Right. So … do you think there might be a computer, some software, that would allow me to make such an archaic thing?"

He shrugged. "Sure. Many hobbyists do similar stuff. Those books have videos in them and 3-D images. I might have some free software around."

"Do I have to pay for the recipes?"

Another odd look came her way. "No. They are on the computer."

"And by that, you mean, free for anyone to use."

He nodded.

Well, at least she had a place to start.

LIEV RACED HOME, an hour late and fed up. But he knew Lani and Charming needed dinner, and they were a long way from being self-sufficient. Besides, caring for Lani was one of the highlights of his day. He hoped he didn't have to be physically at work too many more times, but the messes accumulated if he didn't show up.

The kitchen was buzzing when he walked in. He stopped in shock. All three were in the kitchen. And, if his eyes didn't deceive him, he was pretty sure they were … cooking? Interesting way to act on a holiday. Then again, it's when people often had time to try a new hobby. It also appeared that Milo had shifted the kitchen to mimic theirs at home. It was easy enough to do. And if he'd locked it in, then they could access their kitchen contents from here by opening a cupboard and reaching for the item they wanted. It also meant they could send their new purchases bought while on holiday in their house from here. Made traveling so much easier.

That would likely blow Lani's mind.

A little hard to tell as Milo was trying to show Lani the just-add-water food, and the look on her face would have made Liev fall in love with her if he wasn't already. She looked like she was about to upchuck. She shuddered and turned away. "There's food in the fridge. We can make sandwiches, if nothing else."

"Why bother? That's just as bad for you as this instant stuff. You should just have shakes and be done with it. I'm not hungry. I haven't been hungry in hours."

Liev didn't let anyone know he was here. He was too fascinated at this unique view of the family dynamics in his absence.

Milo brought other boxes of brightly colored instant food out of the cupboard. "You know this stuff was good enough for Liev before you came. Why isn't it good enough for you?"

Liev followed Lani's and the cat's movements. When Lani almost crawled into the fridge, looking for something edible, the sight of her delightful rear end pleased Liev immensely. Then Charming sidled closer to the fridge, and, in a loud whisper directed at Lani, said, "Don't listen to him. Anything that comes in a box can't be good."

She backed up slowly, her arms full, her hair flying everywhere as she tried to maneuver out of the cooler. "Don't worry, Charming. I won't be eating that stuff. Now you, on the other hand …"

"Ha." Charming turned, rose up on his hind legs, and batted a cupboard above his head. The almost-impossible-to-see door opened, revealing stacks of canned cat food. "I'm stocked up."

"Wow. It that all just for you?"

Lani tried to peer into the cupboard, but Charming stood in front, his front legs outstretched and his head moving to stay in her face so she couldn't see. "Yes. It's all mine. Just in case the end of the world comes."

She giggled. "Charming, at the rate you eat, these won't last you one week."

He glanced at the cupboard fearfully. "Really?" And Lani snatched a couple cans while he wasn't looking.

"Hey, those are mine."

"They are canned salmon. Not cat food. *Canned salmon*—people food." She read the label off to him and then held it up, so he could read it himself. Something he was incredibly proficient at.

"Hey, I ordered that for me."

She stopped and stared, but Liev noticed she didn't put the cans back. "You know how to order stuff?"

It was his turn to stare. "Hell yeah."

"Don't swear," she said absentmindedly. "Can you show me how?"

A crafty look came over his face. "If you put the cans back."

She hesitated, obviously torn, and Liev understood something he'd missed up until now. Although her needs had all been met, she hadn't had much choice. She hadn't been able to peruse the shops and order something she wanted. Hell, he'd designed her clothing for her at home and hadn't even considered there might be something else she'd like for herself.

He couldn't remember even asking. He'd been so wrapped up in taking care of her that he'd forgotten to ask what she wanted.

That was something he'd fix. But, for the moment, he wouldn't do anything to disturb this comic relief playing out in front of him. It was exactly what he needed at the end of a shitty day.

CHAPTER 8

"**I** NEED BOTH these cans," Lani scolded. "Don't be greedy. We can order you some more."

His flat face scrunched up, and he said in a pitiful voice, "What if the end of the world comes before it gets here?"

She rolled her eyes. "Like that'll be an issue. Deliveries are almost instantaneous here."

He gave her a fat grin. "Then order your own, and it will be here in time for you to eat it for your dinner."

She glared at him, loving and hating that her cat could argue her into circles. "I'm making something simple for Liev. He's had a tough day, and I want to do something for him tonight."

Charming gave a big nod of approval. "I like the idea of you making food. But you can have one of Milo's shakes and just use a single can for Liev."

She glared, spun around, and slammed the cans onto the counter. "I'm taking two."

"Greedy," Charming muttered. But he immediately headed to the kitchen comp, pulled up the big 3-D monitor, and started pressing the holoscreen with his fat paw. Milo sat open-mouthed throughout the whole thing.

Lani lifted her head and saw Liev partially turned to where Charming had been. He must have heard at least part of the argument with Charming, and she was sure a heated bright pink rolled across her face.

As she watched Liev's shoulders shake as he tried to contain his mirth, it bubbled up and out to bounce across the room.

"Well, I'm glad someone enjoyed that," she muttered.

Liev strode across the short distance, snatched her into his arms, and twirled her around. When he put her back on her feet, he reached up, cupped her cheeks, and gave her a resounding kiss.

When she was free again, Lani laughed. "And here I was thinking you must have had a crappy day, and I was trying to do something nice for you." She pointed to the cans of salmon on the counter. She glanced down at them and froze. Damn it. She spun around, pointing her hand at her cat. "Charming, put that can back."

He slammed the cupboard shut and turned to glare at her. "That's what I was trying to do." His head high, he hopped off the counter and stalked to the big chair in the living room. She swore she heard him mutter, *Thief,* as he passed her.

She groaned. "Is this what a mom with little kids at home feels like while the daddy is at work?"

Liev chuckled. "Probably. Although that scenario is likely not as much fun as this one." He gave her a second kiss. "And thank you for thinking about dinner. We can have salmon sandwiches if you'd like, but I did pick up something to bring home." He motioned to the box on the floor.

Charming's head popped up over the top of the chair. "Food?" He bolted in the direction of the box, beating Liev by seconds. Charming rubbed all along the sides, his nose in the air. "I can't smell anything."

"That's because it's in a special case." Liev lifted it and carried it to the table. He did something that made audible *click*s and removed the lid.

Lani gasped. "Oh my. What is that?"

"It's roast beef with all the vegetables." He smiled at the look of awe on her face. "When I realized I'd be late, I ordered this to come home with me."

She smiled. "It smells heavenly and sure beats take-out as I know it."

Liev pulled out plates and cutlery, then proceeded to serve the ready meal.

Charming danced in his place, his eyes glowing with eagerness. Lani got up, walked to the counter, grabbed the lone can of salmon, and placed it on his plate. "There. You wanted it. Now you can have it."

LIEV LOVED IT.

He could watch Lani and Charming for hours. A warm rosy glow filled his heart. This was the family he hadn't realized he wanted—needed.

They'd just finished dinner when the wall unit beeped, indicating a call. He turned to check the caller. "Stephen."

He walked over to the circle, turned on privacy mode, and answered the call. Lani and Milo cleared the table, one eye on the conversation. Lani couldn't hear the conversation unless Milo let her. Liev made a quick motion, so his brother would do just that. With the two of them listening in, out of the sight of the screen, Liev said, "It's nice to see you, Stephen, but given the lateness of the hour, I gather something is wrong. So what's up?"

"Your number has been coming up as having restricted searches going on and bouncing off our firewalls."

Liev frowned. For one, no need to do that as both he and Milo were perfectly capable of bypassing any of the government firewalls to search for any information they wanted, yet this could be part of the trouble they had earlier. "That doesn't sound right."

"I know. Like you guys would make that mistake, right?" Stephen ran a tired hand over his face. "I guess I'm thinking this might be Lani attracting attention without realizing what she was doing. I'd hoped she'd caught up with our technology and our laws by now after living with you two but maybe not yet. It's a lot to assimilate."

Liev shook his head. "She's not quite there and

most likely was looking for something that she had no idea would cause alarms."

"I'm sorry, but they do cause alarms," Stephen said, spreading his arms. "How damaging could it possibly be to have people learn that our ancestors celebrated holidays, religious and otherwise?" He shook his head. "It boggles the mind to think they felt it was so dangerous that no one should be allowed to know about it."

A contemplative look filtered across Stephen's face. He leaned back and said slowly, "The thing is, although taking a look at that issue is on the agenda down the road, it's not today's problems. And those are much bigger." He tilted his fingers under his chin and continued to work through his thoughts out loud. "Maybe down the road I could use someone like Lani to go through the archives and sort out what information is dangerous and what isn't, based on her unique upbringing. That would at least cut down on the billions of files for the panel to make a final decision on." He laughed. "Right now my problem is actually pulling together a panel. When I got into this, I had no idea what kind of mess I'd be taking on."

Stephen's face broke into a wreath of smiles. "There she is. Hi, Lani."

Liev was startled when an arm slipped around his waist, and Lani stepped into the circle. He always tried to keep her out of the political scene, but, after putting herself front and center during the last debacle with the old Council, and in such smashing style, she'd made history herself.

"Hi, Stephen. How nice to see you." She beamed up at him. "And I accept."

Stephen frowned in confusion, then his face cleared as he understood what she was talking about. "Good," he said, his eyebrows raised in surprise. "Great actually. It can't be today or tomorrow, but it'll be in a couple months. I'll call you in and see about setting up security for you …" He stopped and laughed. "Forget that last part. Liev's company now keeps the security intact. He can set you up with the archives. Just not yet," he rushed to warn her. "I'm in a bit of a pickle right now."

"I'm sorry if I helped cause that pickle," she murmured. "I was looking back on some of the history I hadn't learned about and started searching for information to help fill the gaps." She added in more formal tones, "My apologies."

Stephen shook his head. "No worries. I'll mark this down, and I'll get back to you about our archives in a few weeks." He grinned. "That would be an excellent way for you to fill in the gaps of your education legally." And, with that, he rang off.

CHAPTER 9

THE SECURITY FIELD around her disappeared as Liev closed down the system. She wasn't sure of his reaction to her butting into his session or the work she'd agreed to take on. She'd had Milo's help, and she'd done what she felt was right, so why did she feel like she'd done something wrong?

Because, of course, she had brushed up against personal and government restrictions. "I'm sorry," she said abruptly.

Liev shook his head and tugged her into his arms. "Don't be," he said. He dropped his chin on top of her head. "It's minor in the scheme of things that could go wrong and highlights an inherent issue with the way the government has controlled the flow of information from the public."

Damn right. "And they need to stop it."

"Great volunteering to take on the archives, Lani," Milo said, admiration and maybe a hint of jealousy in his voice. "It will be a heck of a way for you to get comfortable with our system."

She nodded. "A system that is wrong in its current form."

Liev looked down at her. "And because it's wrong, you'll champion it into being right?"

"Someone has to." She smiled up at him. "Since it won't be for a few weeks to a few months, that should give me enough time to get caught up on the missing information I need to know."

"I can help too," Charming said. "You can work from home, and, between us, we can figure out their problems."

Liev rolled his eyes, but Lani was nodding. "That's a good point. Only the two of us know how controlling your society has become. There was some secret stuff way back when, and hackers got into most of it, but that was nothing like the things you guys seem to have deemed dangerous."

"That you know of. Maybe more will be in there than you want to know."

"Maybe." She wasn't concerned. "I also wanted to do something that would help me fit in." She grinned. "Being raised in and having escaped the slaughter of the Naturals makes for a great cover."

"And helps you to better connect to Stephen, as he's in the same boat."

She pondered that. "Then I think my education about the Naturals needs to be beefed up, so I under-stand what he's talking about, if he brings it up."

"That's a great idea." Liev looked to Milo. "Can you make the adjustments to her program?"

"Absolutely," Milo said with a wide grin. "This will

be great. Now we'll have an inside man in the government." At Lani's confused look, he added, "Or should I say, inside *woman*."

LATER THAT NIGHT, Liev, knowing how tired Lani had been earlier on, nudged her to bed. Charming had left them a long time ago, preferring to crash on his Pacific island hammock in the bedroom with the glass floor, so he could dream of all the fish beneath him. Liev wasn't sure what he'd do with one if he actually caught it. It wasn't like it came ready prepped in a can.

Speaking of which, he needed to remember to cancel Charming's earlier order of salmon. Knowing that cat, he had likely gone overboard and ordered dozens of cans to make sure he survived a little longer. Liev shook his head. Talk about an end-of-the-world mentality.

Lani yawned when she came out of the bathroom. She walked to the far end of the bed and crashed.

He'd hoped for a little time alone with her. Just the two of them. Instead, she appeared to be ready to sleep. She flipped onto her back, then rolled to her side. He smiled and crawled in beside her. He could fix this.

She turned into his arms, her lips already reaching for him. He was a lucky man.

He kissed her with all the emotion he felt for her welling up inside him. She responded immediately. It had always been that way between them. Right from their first kiss.

His hands caressed her, like the precious gift she was, only she wasn't having any of it. She shifted restlessly, pressing against him, a whimper catching at the back of her throat. Then she wrapped a leg around him and thrust upward. Oh, Lord, she was killing him. No, she was bringing him to life.

"Love me," she choked out. "Love me now."

Her words hit him in the heart. She was like a furnace, and he was the fire inside her. He shuddered, then reached down to tug her hips into a better position. He pulled down his pants and kicked them off, then eased into her, slowly, achingly, hearing her moan as he filled her.

Heat rolled through him, swamped him. He loved her so much. She called out his name, then pulled his head down and gave him the hottest of kisses.

Damn. He never wanted this to stop, never ever, ever, but he couldn't stop the need driving him forward. He drew back, just an inch.

"No!" she cried out. "Don't pull away."

"*Shhh*. It's too fast," he said. "I have no control tonight."

Her laughter was wild, as wild as he felt inside, with the passion consuming him.

"Can't you see?" Her eyes were bright, her cheeks flushed. She wrapped her arms around his shoulders, pulling him down against her. "Neither do I."

The fire inside him blazed, and he made a noise he

didn't recognize. Primitive. Possessive. Passionate. Unable to hold back, he plunged once, twice, and once more. She called out his name as she pulsed against him, around him, then called out his name again.

He was a goner, losing control. He threw his head back as he came apart, rejoicing in her cries beneath him, until her cries died down, and he fell into her embrace. Both of them shuddered with emotion and completion and the wonder of their love. They stayed like that for minutes, their breaths slowing, holding each other tightly, a sheen of sweat on their bodies, not ready to let go.

"I love you." Her voice was languid and sleepy, her body relaxed.

"You're my heart," he said and kissed her tenderly.

"*Mmmm.*" She was half asleep in his arms.

He let her go, and she snuggled onto her side of the bed, her breaths slow and steady. With a gentle smile, he eased to the side, then tucked her in.

She was exhausted.

He, on the other hand, was wide awake. Happy. Invigorated.

And he wasn't quite ready to sleep.

He walked back out to the living room and brought up the main computer.

Considering Stephen's earlier call, he hacked his way into the government databanks and behind their privacy laws and security guards. There he searched out the information Lani had been looking for. Though he didn't understand why she'd search for something she'd already experienced many times over.

As he read through the information, he shook his head at the government. Anything religious had been locked up. Except that Christmas apparently only had a religious overtone for some people. The others had taken to it as a fun celebration.

He checked his mail and made sure there were no new issues at work. Just as he was about to close down the computer, he noticed the symbol on the top right corner. *Saved searches.* He frowned. He hadn't searched for anything recently and never saved them. One never knew when a system would get hacked. In fact, the computers deleted all information and ghosted all tracks at the end of the day. That was the standard operating procedure. Wondering what Lani was up to, he clicked on her saved searches and sat back with a heavy sigh.

She was missing her old life. Here was evidence. She'd spent hours trying to find things like Christmas trees, decorations, LED lights—whatever they were. Bringing up the other government information, he cross-referenced the information so he could see what she was looking for and why. When he was finally done, an idea formed in the back of his head.

But was it a good one? If she wanted to do something, did she want to do it alone?

And, if he stepped in, would that ruin it for her?

CHAPTER 10

L ANI WOKE EARLY the next morning, but the household was already up and busy. She wandered into the kitchen in search of coffee—and found Milo and Liev wearing business suits. She stopped. "Going somewhere?"

Liev looked up, saw her, and walked over to kiss her good morning. "Hey. Sorry, we both have an early morning meeting."

She nodded. "Okay. How long will you be?"

She hated to be alone in his world, but this gave her the freedom to work on her gift for Liev. She didn't have anything for Milo and couldn't even begin to imagine what she could give him either. But, when she saw him and his shiny black pants with almost glow-in-the-dark white dots on them and his orange mohawk, she had the beginnings of an idea, ... if she could find what she needed.

That only left Charming to find something for. And that was minor. With his endless stomach, anything food-oriented would be perfect.

And, while the two were gone, she and Charming could work this ordering system just fine.

She smiled up at Liev. "Feels very homey, sending you off to do a day's work."

He grinned that lopsided grin of his. "It had better not be all day. I expect that Milo will be home in a couple hours, and I'll be home by midafternoon." He hesitated, glanced around the room, and said, "If you need anything …"

"We'll be fine," she said, pointing to the portal. "Go. Take care of business, and come home when you can. We'll be fine."

A small frown of concern appeared on his forehead, but he dropped a second kiss on her lips and walked through the portal. Milo waved at the two of them and followed his brother to the office.

Lani picked up Charming and danced around the room. "We're alone."

"And …?"

She laughed, plunked him on the counter, and poured a huge mug of coffee. "I have plans, and you are needed to make them all happen."

He preened. "Of course. That makes perfect sense."

And because he was such a perfect ass of a cat, she poured him some cream too. Then she picked up her coffee and said, "Follow me."

It took him about twenty minutes to figure out her cookbook stuff, and, before long, she was copying recipes that she remembered from her childhood—or rather recipes that sounded like the ones she had had as a kid—putting them into a book program, and voila!

She ran to the bedroom where Liev had set up a temporary office, a room that housed the printer while on vacation.

"Oh, my God. The book is on material." She held up the cloth item and shook her head. "This is not what I want."

"At least it's washable that way," he said with irrefutable logic.

"True, but I want paper, or whatever passes for paper in this time, with lots of glossy photos."

Charming looked at the printer, made a few adjustments, and back they went to the main computer. It took four more tries before she got something even close to what she wanted. And then, while proofing it, she found several errors and had to fix those. When the final product was in her hand, she laughed and ran outside to sit in the sun and to look at it. "Thanks, Charming. It's exactly what I wanted."

"Yeah, but you said it was for him." He rubbed against her. "Why would he want that? Besides, it's not like any good recipes are in there for me."

She grinned. "Ah, but now I'm not limited. I can do what I want and create as many of these as I want."

He sprawled on the deck beside her. "As you wish." And he promptly fell asleep.

Crap. She needed to know more about the ordering stuff. As she glanced at him, she realized she could work on some of it alone. The men could be home at any time, and she desperately wanted to hide the evidence of their work. She ran back inside, hid the book with her clothing, and dashed to the computer to write down the rest of her instructions, so she could recreate her morning's work later. Feeling as if she had accomplished a lot, she cleared the computer's memory.

It took a few moments before she realized she was in the clear. Except … for the failures. The projects that hadn't worked out so well.

She ran to throw everything into the recycler. Just as she was done, both Milo and Liev strolled back in. She stood with her hands behind her back and wiped the guilty look off her face.

She hoped.

LIEV EYED HER in amusement as he walked toward her. He had no idea what she was up to, and that was fine. She was entitled to her privacy.

But he was curious. His gaze was drawn to the recycler and the flashing lights on the side. Something she'd put in there was being processed—just not very well. Then again, she had little experience with recycler jams. Still, to point it out to her now would be awkward and might destroy whatever surprise she had been planning. He kissed her lightly. "I'll get changed, then prepare us some food. I'm starving."

She backed away and took a quick glance in the direction of the bedroom. His curiosity ramped up another notch.

He went into the room and shut the door. After a quick shower to help wash away the distaste from his last meeting, he finally walked through the bedroom looking for new clothes. He couldn't stop himself from looking around, wondering what she was up to. Her face was too open to hide anything. He reminded himself it was her secret, and he'd have to wait until she was ready to share.

He walked to the kitchen and pulled sandwich fixings from the fridge. Neither Milo nor Lani were around. He frowned, checked the time, and reassured himself he hadn't been gone that long. He walked outside to the deck, sure that Lani must have gone to her favorite spot, the hammock. Instead it was empty too. Worried, he walked through the place, looking for his family.

Ten minutes later, he was frantically punching codes on the locators to find out where Lani and Milo had gone.

And where the hell was Charming?

That damn flashing light on the recycler caught his eye as he stormed past. He opened the machine and out popped Charming, spitting and hissing, like the cat he was.

"Charming!" He heard the alarm in his voice. "What happened to you, and where are Lani and Milo?"

Charming hopped to his back feet, his front paws

punching air and his eyes glittering with temper. "A bot took them. Walked right into the kitchen, didn't even say a word. He just threw something around Lani and Milo, and, the next thing I know, he'd shoved me in there." Charming spun around and glared at the recycler. "He could have killed me."

Liev stared at the machine and then at Charming. The whole point was to kill him. Clean up so no one was left behind to set up an alarm about the missing two. They hadn't known that Liev was here. Now was this a sanctioned ComBot, or was this something else again? He strode to the holo unit on the wall, put it in secrecy mode, and called Stephen. When his buddy's tired face came on, Liev quickly explained.

Thankfully Stephen started punching numbers, then shook his head. "It's not us. We don't have an order in place to pick up either of them."

Signing off, Liev went to the big kitchen computer Milo had set up in the rental and turned on the trackers. Damn. According to this, Lani and Milo were still on the island. He stared outside, sorting this out. Why would anyone come here, take prisoners, and not leave the island?

Unless they were waiting for Liev to show up.

Shit.

Chapter 11

L ANI COULD SPIT, she was so mad. How could Liev and Milo have such advanced technology and yet be so prone to break-ins? It was one thing if this was a government-sanctioned raid and retrieval, but it wasn't. No way this guy was legal. Hell, he wasn't even human. Or was he?

She eyed him closely. He appeared to be a cross between a bot and a man. Big beer gut with a mechanical hand—maybe two mechanical hands. She couldn't tell with the other one. And he was big. Surely no human would have taken Charming and dumped him in the recycler, like this bot had done. That was just wrong. The only reason she wasn't in full-blown panic at the thought was because she had seen that it was jammed. At the time, she'd been more concerned that Liev would be the one to notice and try to unjam it, but now she had bigger things to worry about. Like this asshole.

And then there was this weird location. Like inside a really badly designed cabin, where the builder had run out of materials. It kind of matched the kidnapper.

Milo asked in a mild voice, "What do you want?"

"Money, of course."

Milo raised an eyebrow. "And how will this help you get it?"

Lani wanted to laugh. Their kidnapper had tried to kill Charming, and that talking cat was worth a fortune. This guy wasn't too bright. "Who are you?"

"Buck's the name. And make-a-buck is what I do."

She stared at him. Surely he didn't mean making little bucks because that was just gross. The man was a mountain of bits and pieces and, from the looks of it, android bit and pieces. Nothing was attractive about him with his huge bald head and grimy beard that fell to the middle of his oversize paunch. Maybe her feelings showed on her face, because he snarled, "What's the matter? Never seen anyone make an honest living before?"

She reared back. "An *honest* living? Is that what you call kidnapping?"

"Sure. Hell, if you rich folk weren't so busy ordering stuff all the time, we wouldn't be able to track you, would we? Huh? Think I don't know you're stockpiling for some event? Well, I don't need much, but I can resell anything that you do have. Takes me nothing to turn a buck on the black market."

She had no idea what he was talking about. "So why are we here if you wanted stuff from inside the house?"

"Ha. Because I figured that, with you two out of the way, I could go back and see what else you might have there that I could use. I saw some mighty fine electronics."

Milo bristled.

"Yours, huh?" Buck grinned. "And, if you've got

that kind of equipment, then you've got money. And, if you've got money, then I want some."

"Then take us back," Lani said, "and we'll give you the little bit we have."

She was desperate to rescue Charming. And she had a little money—not that she was into paying for blackmail or kidnappings. Besides, shouldn't Milo have protection from guys like this? She eyed Buck suspiciously. "Who do you work for?"

He snorted. "Why would I work for anyone? I'd have to share the profits then, wouldn't I?"

Good point. And she didn't think, from the looks of him, that he was doing too well in this business. She watched Milo as he studied him. Evidently the man didn't pass muster because Milo turned away in disgust. Yet she and Milo were both chained by something odd. Buck had thrown this loop around them in the kitchen, and that had been it. He'd yanked, and they'd been transported here.

Wherever *here* was.

She managed to press the buttons that she could feel ever-so-subtly under her skin. One should be an alarm for Liev to find her. She was actually surprised he hadn't already arrived. Then again, he didn't know where they were. Maybe this was a different planet for all she knew. He also might not know yet they were missing.

"So let us go. We'll all go back home, and you can take anything you can carry."

He glared at her. "That's likely to be a trap."

"What?" She shook her head. "How can it be a trap? We're both here."

He pondered the issue. "Nah, I'll return alone. Scope out your stuff, figure out how to move it all, and then come back here for you."

"Wait. Where are we?" she asked, hearing the urgency in her voice. Now that he was ready to disappear, she was afraid of being left alone forever. They'd die like this.

"Ha." He smirked. "That's for me to know and for you to find out."

Then he lifted his wrist unit, fiddled with the dials, and appeared to vaporize in front of them.

She turned to face Milo. "Any great ideas of how to get out of this mess?"

He nodded. "Maybe. But we need to get free first."

"Great. And how do we do that?"

He shrugged. "No freakin' clue."

LIEV WATCHED LANI'S trail end in the middle of what was supposed to be a large open field at the edge of the beach. He stood here, tracker in hand, and studied the empty spot. He shook his tracker, just to make sure it hadn't somehow been damaged. But it still read that Lani and Milo were both in front of him. He frowned and considered the options. If they were here, as the instrument in his hands said, then they were under some kind of camouflage. He knew that a lot of thieves used a similar device. Liev had had no need for one, so he hadn't looked into it any further. Now he realized he should have. Knowing the enemy's equipment was standard advice for anyone. Given that he was in the security business, it was even more important. He sighed. There'd never been enough time.

And how about now?

He could almost hear Milo's mocking voice. Liev had to presume that they were here in front of him, but he couldn't see them. Was their kidnapper with them? And was it one man, like Charming had said, or were more here helping him? Neither were great options.

The thought of Charming alone in the house worried away at the back of his mind.

If the kidnapper returned to the house, he just might kill Charming this time. The cat had already ended up in the recycler, so round one had gone to the bad guy.

Charming wanted a rematch, but was he in a position to beat someone like this? Plus, if the kidnapper figured out that Charming could talk, then he'd become one of the stolen goods.

Liev lifted his communicator and whispered to Charming, "You there?"

"I'm here. Weird sounds coming from the other part of the house though."

Ah, shit. The kidnapper had come back, probably to clean out the place. Liev didn't give a damn about the equipment. Milo had everything set so the equipment would self-destruct if it left the property without a special password.

Still, Liev didn't dare let anything happen to Charming. Lani would kill him if that happened, but neither could he leave his wife and brother in the kidnapper's clutches.

"Stay hidden," he ordered Charming. "I'm going to see if I can find Lani."

"I thought you already did that," Charming snapped. "You've been gone for at least twenty minutes, and the locator led you right to her. What have you been doing all this time?"

In the small screen of the communicator, Charming gasped, turned to face the doorway, and went quiet for a long moment, long enough to worry Liev. Finally he turned back to face the communicator. Anger rippled through his orange fur. "I think the kidnapper is in the kitchen."

"Charming, stay away from him," Liev said in alarm. "Hide somewhere safe. He dumped you in the recycler once. Remember? Next time he's likely to kill you outright." Damn. Liev hated being torn like this. With one more warning for Charming, he said, "And, for God's sake, don't let him know you can talk."

Charming's angry face peered into the communicator. "I won't. You get Lani and get back here."

And he disappeared from view.

Chapter 12

LANI KNEW IT would be only a matter of time before Liev found them. But that didn't mean Liev had found Charming. This Buck asshole would also return soon. Potentially with everything he wanted from the house. Just as scary was the fact that he could surprise an unknowing Liev. And that wouldn't be good either. If they were all captured, no one but Charming was left behind.

Stuck in the recycler.

She tried to think of a way to get out of this damn lasso. "Milo, surely you have something to disrupt the electrical wave on this stupid tie-down strap."

Milo turned to stare at her. "What would that do? We'd still be tied up."

"Would we? Without the current, wouldn't this thing drop to the floor?"

He snorted. "It's not the current. This is memory cord, and, even when disconnected from the source, it will hold its position."

Damn. Was nothing ever easy here? "Then hack it."

He groaned and dropped his head backward. "And how do you expect me to do that?"

"How the hell should I know? I don't want to just sit here."

"Why not?" He closed his eyes and added, "Liev will be here soon."

"And what if this asshole surprises Liev and catches him too?"

Milo froze, then relaxed. "Nah, Liev is too smart for that."

She hoped so, but this was damn irritating. "Are you really saying that, with your bag of tricks, you can't get us out of here?" When Milo stayed silent, she couldn't help but needle him and that competitive part of him. "Bet Charming would find a way."

She watched Milo's placid look fire up into outrage. "Hey, that's not fair."

She shrugged and waited. When she glanced over again, he was assessing the loops around his chest and shoulders, then the big square block in the center of the shack. She wasn't even sure they were inside a building. "Any idea where we are?" she asked out loud.

"How can I figure this out if you keep talking?" he said.

"Oops," she murmured but smiled and sat back. Her wrist started to flash. "My communicator is going off," she said. With a sigh, he turned to look at her, saw the same lights as she did, and raised an eyebrow. Then a crafty look came into his gaze. "Told you that Liev would find us."

"Maybe and maybe not." She couldn't help worrying. "What if it's Charming?"

"And what's wrong with that?"

"Maybe Liev is still in trouble." She sighed and wished Milo would move that incredible brain of his in the direction of getting them out of here.

She opened her eyes and idly studied the room. It almost looked like a tent but with some support at the lower portion of the wall. Except … she leaned forward. "Is that trees and water I see?"

Milo turned to look the same direction and whistled. "This is a camouflage unit."

"Yeah, like I know what that means," she muttered.

"It means, Liev won't see us, even if he is looking for us."

"What?" she cried out. "How do we tell him then?"

Milo, as if finally considering this to be serious enough to warrant his full attention, nodded to the weird box in the middle. "That's keeping the camouflage in place."

"So …" She really wondered if boy genius here was that smart sometimes. "How do we put it out of commission?" She struggled to free herself, but, no matter what she did, the ties kept her arms bound at her side and her feet in place. She tried to hop forward and managed to move slightly, then the ties seemed to understand what she was trying to do and stopped her. "Is this stuff like intelligent or something?"

"Yeah. That's what makes it so special. You can do something once, but then it learns."

"Great." Giving it some thought, she relaxed completely, as much as anyone tied up in the middle of some kidnapping mess. She felt the ties relax. Counting slowly to three, she swung her arms in front and held them straight out. The ties immediately pulled them back to her body, but … just the upper half of her arm. She now had the use of her lower arms and her wrists. And that meant her communicator.

She quickly turned it on. Sensing Milo's interest, she focused on calling Liev.

"Lani?"

"Yes! Milo and I are in some kind of special camouflage unit and tied with a strange cord that won't let us go." She took a deep breath and tried to control the excitement threatening to raise her voice. "I have no idea where we are, but you have to help Charming. The asshole who kidnapped us stuffed him in the recycler."

"He's out, and he's fine." Liev's voice deepened. "The kidnapper is in the house now, so I don't know who to feel sorry for—Charming or the kidnapper."

Lani gasped. "Oh, no. I have to go save him."

"Hang on," Liev said. "I think I'm seeing something here."

Lani turned to see Milo doing something weird with his locator unit on his wrist. She knew hers was a plain Jane locator, but she'd never seen Milo's in action. A weird glow surrounded his whole arm.

"Milo's doing something, but I have no idea what. His arm is glowing blue."

"Oh, perfect."

"Perfect?" As much as she loved these two guys, they really needed to work a little more on their damn explanations.

"He's required his unit to go to maximum power, and, when that happens, his unit will go to the closest power source and drain it."

"Oh." Even the expanded explanation didn't help much. She watched as the walls wavered, then sparks flew, and suddenly their ties dropped, and the tent mirage disappeared. She spun around.

And there was Liev. They were standing in the field by the beach, only ten minutes from the house.

She laughed and ran into Liev's open arms.

CHARMING WAITED AROUND the corner. He had the computer up, with the video on, to make sure he had something to show for his efforts. He wouldn't let this guy take anything of his. Maybe something from the others. They had lots. He, on the other hand, didn't, and he needed everything he had. And more.

He crouched low, out of sight, and watched the intruder search the premises. He eyed the electronics. That couldn't be good. How could Charming order more food if this guy interrupted the supply chain?

A strange rumble filled the small house.

The hair on his spine stood up straight, and he

hunkered lower.

Then a huge crate appeared in the kitchen.

"Woot! Now this is more like it," the intruder crowed, as he walked around the crate. "This is the order I was alerted to. Now … what is it?"

Charming's gaze went to the symbol he finally noticed at the bottom corner of the crate.

Shock and horror filled him. Then came the anger.

He searched the area around him. And spied the automatic tape thingy they'd used to wrap Lani's gifts for the brothers.

Charming grinned. That crate was his order. And no one—especially this intruder—would steal from him.

"THANK YOU SO much." Lani smiled up at him. "I hated being tied up."

"Thank Milo," Liev said. "He figured out how to destroy the mirage."

He was right. She'd been frustrated with Milo's acceptance of the situation, but, once he'd focused on the problem, wow.

"Then again, Lani prodded me into it. She wasn't into waiting for you to show up and save her." Milo ran past them. "She's a pain in the ass most of the time."

"Love you too," she yelled. But he was either too far away to hear or couldn't be bothered to answer.

"Not as much as I love you." Liev grabbed her hand. "Now let's go stop this asshole."

They raced up behind Milo, who had stopped just outside the house, his head turned to hear better. Liev kept Lani slightly behind him as they approached. "Milo, what do you hear?"

Milo snorted. "Listen for yourself."

Liev turned his head to hear better but didn't need to. Damn if a male wasn't screaming and hollering for help. "What the hell?"

Lani gasped. "Charming!" She ran past the other two.

"Lani, wait!" Liev raced after her. Damn that girl. She always raced in where angels feared to tread, and the minute anything was wrong with Charming, she was there for him.

Then again, that was one of the things he loved about her. She'd do the same for him and Milo too. They were a family—as she'd often pointed out—and family took care of their own.

With Milo alongside him, Liev closed the distance between them, just managing to catch Lani before she rushed inside. "Wait. Let's do this the smart way."

Frantic, she tried to pull her arm free. "I have to help Charming."

Milo grabbed her head and forcibly turned her so she could see into the kitchen.

She gasped and immediately froze as she tried to fully understand what she saw.

Hell. Liev studied the nightmare in front of him, and even he didn't get it.

Then it hit him.

He'd forgotten to cancel Charming's order. That had likely been what had triggered this guy to find their house as a potential target in the first place. Large orders were often trouble. As they'd found out.

But he doubted this asshole would try this stunt again.

He shook his head, took another look, and started laughing.

Chapter 13

L ANI STARED AROUND the kitchen, her mind still grasping the reality before her.

The kidnapper was on the floor, wrapped up in packing tape. He was so crazily bound that he was in a half-sitting, half-lying position, with one knee up to his chest and his arms crossed over his massive chest.

"What the …?"

The kitchen was overwhelmed with cans, as if the large crate had burst open, and the cans had sprung free and had spread far and wide.

"Serves you right. I hope they put you away for ten years," snapped Charming, sitting on top of the crate with one side blown open. "You're a thief, and no one steals from me."

"Charming, did you do that?"

He sniffed, his nose going high into the air. "Of course. Someone had to protect the house. After all, you took off."

"What? That's not fair." She ran and scooped him up and scolded him. "You be nice. I didn't take off. He kidnapped me."

She scratched Charming under the chin and

grinned when his eyes crossed with pleasure.

"If you keep doing that," Charming said with a purr in his voice, "I'll believe you."

"Something attacked me. Help. Help!" cried Buck.

She rounded on him. "Why should I help you? You kidnapped me, stuck poor Charming here in the recycler, and was prepared to clean out the house. You're nothing but a low-down nasty thief."

"Yeah," Charming said. And damn if he didn't hawk up a hairball onto the thief's head. She quickly put Charming down. "That's just gross."

"He deserved it." Her cat hopped back up on top of the crate and proceeded to clean his butt.

She shook her head and watched as Liev and Milo bent over the robber. They removed something, ran it through the computer, then grinned at each other.

"What are you doing?"

"He's an escapee. Wanted for a long list of crimes. And there's a bounty on his head."

"A bounty?"

"That's mine," Charming crowed. "I caught him."

"Like that can happen. You don't have an identity number," she said. "Or a bank account."

He glared at her. "First you steal my salmon, and now you want to take my prize money." He sniffed, turned around, and curled up in a ball. "You guys work it out. After all that hard work, I'm tired."

And he went off to sleep.

Lani turned her attention back to the men and realized that the robber was unconscious. "What did you guys do to him?"

"We're implanting the suggestion that Charming is a new robopet."

She laughed. "That's a great cover actually. He's very *unpetlike*, but, hey, to each his own."

Then they did something else that caused a series of bells and chimes to happen. She stepped closer to Liev as the house almost shook with the vibration. "What's happening?"

"Calling in the ComBots to collect this guy. And, Charming, please don't talk while they are here."

Only snores could be heard from the orange fluff ball.

A flash of bright light filled the house.

Charming woke up, howled, and dashed into the bedroom. Lani wrapped her arms around Liev, trembling with the memories of the last time the ComBots had arrived. This time, however, they were polite and official. They quickly scanned Buck's ID, then scanned Liev's and Milo's, followed by Lani's. She waited nervously, desperately trying not to show it. Liev kept her tucked up close, while the formalities were done. The ComBots grabbed the unconscious Buck, and they were gone. Just like that.

"Wow. I'm glad this process was over quickly because those guys are still scary."

"Not when you are on the right side of the law." Liev turned to his brother. "Milo, do you want to check out the mess that Buck left behind and see if anything is of interest? I'll deal with this crate."

She didn't have a chance to ask what it was, before he had it whisked off to storage. Since they had movable space, they never ran out of room anymore, as the walls could shift to accommodate anything. Even this rental house had that capacity. And to make it even better, according to Liev, by modelling the kitchen here after the one at home, the products would move automatically into the same space at home. So no packing up this haul to take home. She loved that. Need a bigger closet? No problem. Just program it to make it bigger. Or keep stuffing it, and it grew intuitively.

She turned when she realized that she and Liev were alone again. Finally.

She ran into his arms and hugged him close.

"I'm sure glad you know how this world works," she said against his lips before she gave him a blazing kiss.

He laughed and said, "Me too. But I wish I knew how *your* world worked."

LATER THAT NIGHT, with Lani tucked up close to him, he realized he understood very little of how Lani's world had worked. What mattered back then? What did her society believe to be worth fighting for?

He slipped out of bed and walked out to the living room computer. And found Milo already on the unit. His kid brother looked up, a guilty look on his face.

Liev walked over, took a closer look at what he was doing, and laughed and laughed. "That's what I came out to do."

The two bent their heads together and got to work.

Chapter 14

S EVERAL DAYS LATER, Lani rolled over in bed and stretched. The last few days had been good. Peaceful and loving. In the aftermath of the kidnapping, she'd gone back to being exhausted from all the stress. Still, it was over, and life had slipped back to a normal pattern.

Half dozing, she lay here until finally something odd penetrated her senses. Music. Not that music was odd, but this kind was.

Christmas music. What the …?

She got up and wrapped herself in a warm robe lying on the edge of the bed and then stopped. Gone was the Pacific island cottage. She glanced out the window and gasped. Snow. On the ground, on the trees, and no palm trees were in sight. She ran out to the living room to find Charming skittering in ahead of her. She stared. Was that tinsel clinging to his butt?

She hit the brakes at the living room in shock. The living room was gone. Instead, they were in a huge log cabin with a rock fireplace blazing in front of her. Her stunned gaze traveled from the fire up the fireplace to something that had her hand slapping over her mouth.

Tears crept into her eyes. She dragged her gaze away from full stockings hanging on the mantel to sweeping across the room. A huge tree to the left stood between a large bay window with a window seat and the fireplace. She zipped around to look at the other side to find Milo and Liev, both sporting bright red-and-white Santa caps. She burst into tears, frozen in place. Both men lost their huge grins. Through her tears, she watched Liev take several faltering steps toward her.

"Lani?"

She shook her head, scrubbing her face with the sleeves of her robe.

Charming rubbed down the side of her legs. "Is this for real?" he asked. "Do we get presents?"

She giggled, the sound huskier than usual. "I don't know. Have you been a good boy?"

"I'm the best." He puffed out his chest and strutted. Then he stopped and shot her a worried look. "They contacted Santa, didn't they?"

"Did you write him and tell him what you wanted?" she managed to get out between her giggles.

Charming stopped, his stare frozen on her face. "That was your job. You know that, right? You had one job to do. Did you do it?"

She couldn't hold it in and burst out in big guffaws, her tears gone now. She snagged him up, twirled him around and around, gave him a huge noisy kiss—much to his disgust—dropped him on the window seat, and raced toward Liev.

He laughed and twirled her around, like she had with Charming. When he was done, she still clung to him. "Thank you. Thank you!"

His laughter rumbled up, making her laugh again.

"You're welcome. Besides, we figured that, before you got carried away with ordering stuff, we'd better step in and do it so no one would know."

She turned to look at the tree decorated with tiny lights that twinkled, as if laughing in the dim light. There were tiny miniature carvings, little boxes tied up in bright ribbons. Snowflakes. "Oh my," she whispered. "Where did you find all this? I couldn't get anywhere with my searches."

"Just enough to trigger the bots," Liev teased.

She flushed. "I thought I was being so smart."

"You were. But it might take a little bit before you get the system down pat."

"That's all right. When I want something now, I'll ask for your help." She walked toward the tree. "You did this for me?"

"*We* did this for you."

She glanced at Milo, who looked mildly uncomfortable. She grinned. Then she ran over and hugged him—hard—before racing back to the tree.

"And not for me?" Charming asked in an injured tone.

"Absolutely for you too," she said with a special smile.

"*Humph.*"

And then she caught sight of the presents under the tree. Two of them. For her. One from Milo and one from Liev.

She laughed and raced back to the bedroom, calling behind her, "Wait. I have something to put under the tree too."

She dug through her closet, found the two gifts she'd managed to order with Charming's help, and ran back out to the living room. She was going to put them under the tree but couldn't wait. She headed toward the men and handed them their gifts. "You can open them now."

The looks on their faces were hilarious. They didn't know what to do with the odd packages.

"I had Charming's help," she said, then added with a sheepish grin, "I ran into a little trouble."

Liev opened his first. His look of shock had her rushing into an explanation. "It's a cookbook. Of Christmas recipes. From my time. Or as close as I could come."

His surprise turned to interest. He went to sit down, stopped, and kissed her passionately. "Thank you. It's wonderful!"

She beamed. "You're welcome. I was trying to figure out what to get the guy who can buy everything."

"I think that's one reason they did away with the holidays," Liev said. "It became frustrating once everyone could make everything for themselves."

He spun around as if just remembering and looked

at Milo. "What did you get?"

Milo was turning the package around in his hand. He looked up at Lani and shrugged. "I have no idea."

Yeah, she hadn't been too sure about his gift. "It's a hair paint set."

For the blank look on his face, she walked over, grateful she'd read the instructions on the package, and opened it. Then she took out a large circle, which she held up against his wild red-and-purple swirled pants. She clicked the unit. Then she held the circle up to his mohawk and clicked a second time. There were a few seconds of delay while he stared at her.

Then—*poof!*—his huge mohawk matched the color of his pants.

Liev gasped. He got up and walked around Milo, as Lani repeated her actions on the other side.

"Oh my." Liev howled with laughter.

Milo shot him a dirty look, then walked over to the window. He let out a scream, stared at his reflection in amazement, then turned to stare at her. "Holy yowsers," he whispered, turning once again to stare at his image. "This is the best thing ever."

"I'm glad," she said. "You're a little hard to buy for."

"Well, you found something that he'll drive us nuts with for a long time." Liev came up behind her, his arms sliding around her ribs. "It's so cool though. He'll set a trend with all his other geek friends."

She turned in the circle of his arms. "That's okay

too."

He dropped a kiss on her nose. "Now it's your turn."

He led her over to the chair and sat her down. "Milo, yours or my gift first?"

Milo bounded forward. "Mine," he crowed. He ran to the tree and picked up the smaller of the two gifts and came back with it in his outstretched hands. "For you." After giving her the small packet, he stepped back, bouncing in place.

She turned it over, wondering what kind of tech gadget he'd gotten her. She ripped open the wrapping paper and stared. It was a small black box. She opened it and was no wiser. She raised a questioning look to Milo. "What is it?"

He grinned. "It's enhancements for you."

Her gaze widened, then she squealed, "Really?"

He nodded. "So you can have the tech savvy stuff." He moved an arm to the Christmas tree. "You obviously need them earlier rather than later."

She laughed. "Thank you." She meant it. It had been so frustrating knowing that Charming had gotten the enhancements with their time-travel event that had been meant for her.

Liev stepped up and handed her a larger box. She stared at it. She was so happy to know he'd bought her something that she didn't really care what it was. Then she opened it.

And stared.

"Is it a clothing thing?"

"I realized that I was basically making your clothes, and you had very little input." He sat down beside her and tapped the box. "We'll have to show you how to work this, but now you can make any type of clothing you'd like. Including designing your own styles."

As gifts went, it was pretty special.

"I love it," she whispered.

"Hey, what about me?"

Everyone turned toward Charming. He sat on the window seat, staring at them. There was hope in his eyes but also a sense of disgust. "You guys forgot about me, didn't you?"

"No." Lani grinned. She went back to the bedroom and pulled out the one gift she'd made with needle and thread and an old outfit of hers. She came out holding it in her hands. A tiny vest.

"Oh no. No way I'm wearing that."

She was ready for his resistance. Before he could figure out what she was planning to do, she caught him and wrestled him into the vest.

While the two men looked on, she plunked him back on the window seat. "You look adorable," she said in admiration.

"Ha. I look stupid." But he was sniffing it and admiring himself in the reflective window pane. "At least it's my color."

She laughed. The vest was as orange as Charming was.

"We have something for you as well." Milo went to the far cupboard and pressed a series of codes.

And damn if that huge pallet that the kidnapper had been trying to steal didn't pop out of the wall.

She stood up. "What *is* that?"

"Mine! Mine. Mine!" Charming bolted for the top of those cans. "It's all mine." He did a flip in the air and landed perfectly.

"But what is it?" she exclaimed.

Liev laughed. "It's something you apparently stole from him."

Confused, she stared at the box and shook her head. "I've never stolen anything from Charming." At his snort, she glared at him. "Ever."

"You stole one can." He sat back on his haunches. "I snuck one back and then placed an order all on my own." He cast a wary eye at Liev. "On Liev's account, to replace it."

And dimly she remembered the salmon incident from their attempt at dinner not long ago. "You ordered a *pallet* of salmon because I took one can from the cupboard?"

Not possible. But from the look on his flat face, apparently it was.

And then it clicked. "And that's the order that let the kidnapper realize we must have something worth stealing?"

Liev laughed.

Milo grinned.

Charming snorted. "Like I would let him get away with stealing this. I told you. *No more stealing*." He gave her a huge fat grin. "And now they've given the whole thing to me for Christmas!"

"Oh, Lord," she said in fascination, walking closer. "You can't possibly eat all that yourself."

He reared back on his legs. "Get back. It's mine. All mine." But he misjudged the edge and tumbled backward.

They broke out laughing. Lani walked over and picked him up. "You're so round now that soon you won't be able to climb on top of your stash. If you eat all of this salmon, you'll get fat."

He eyed her, eyed his own healthy-size rump, then dropped his glance back to the pallet. And said, "Okay, you can have one can."

With a snort, he pinned her with his huge orange eyes and added, "But only one!"

He flopped onto his back, threw his arms wide open, and yelled, "Best Christmas ever!"

The End

This concludes Book 4 of Broken Protocols:
Cat's Claus.

Arsenic in the Azaleas

A new cozy mystery series from USA Today best-selling author Dale Mayer. Follow gardener and amateur sleuth Doreen Montgomery—and her amusing and mostly lovable cat, dog, and parrot—as they catch murderers and solve crimes in lovely Kelowna, British Columbia.

Riches to rags. ... Controlling to chaos. ... But murder ... seriously?

After her ex-husband leaves her high and dry, former socialite Doreen Montgomery's chance at a new life comes in the form of her grandmother, Nan's, dilapidated old house in picturesque Kelowna ... and the added job of caring for the animals Nan couldn't take into assisted living with her: Thaddeus, the loquacious African gray parrot with a ripe vocabulary, and his buddy, Goliath, a monster-size cat with an equally monstrous attitude.

It's the new start Doreen and her beloved basset hound, Mugs, desperately need. But, just as things start to look up for Doreen, Goliath the cat and Mugs the dog find a human finger in Nan's overrun garden.

And not just a finger. Once the police start digging, the rest of the body turns up and turns out to be connected to an old unsolved crime.

With her grandmother as the prime suspect, Doreen soon finds herself stumbling over clues and getting on Corporal Mack Moreau's last nerve, as she does her best to prove her beloved Nan innocent of murder.

Arsenic in the Azaleas is available now!
To find out more visit Dale Mayer's website.
https://geni.us/DMArsenicUniversal

Author's Note

Thank you for reading Cat's Claus! If you enjoyed my book, I'd appreciate it if you'd leave a review.

Dear reader,

I love to hear from readers, and you can contact me at my website: www.dalemayer.com or at my Facebook author page. To be informed of new releases and special offers, sign up for my newsletter or follow me on BookBub. And if you are interested in joining Dale Mayer's Reader Group, here is the Facebook sign up page.
http://geni.us/DaleMayerFBGroup

Cheers,
Dale Mayer

About the Author

Dale Mayer is a *USA Today* best-selling author, best known for her SEALs military romances, her Psychic Visions series, and her Lovely Lethal Garden cozy series. Her contemporary romances are raw and full of passion and emotion (Broken But … Mending, Hathaway House series). Her thrillers will keep you guessing (Kate Morgan, By Death series), and her romantic comedies will keep you giggling (*It's a Dog's Life*, a stand-alone novella; and the Broken Protocols series, starring Charming Marvin, the cat).

Dale honors the stories that come to her—and some of them are crazy, break all the rules and cross multiple genres!

To go with her fiction, she also writes nonfiction in many different fields, with books available on résumé writing, companion gardening, and the US mortgage system. All her books are available in print and ebook format.

Connect with Dale Mayer Online

Dale's Website – www.dalemayer.com
Twitter – @DaleMayer
Facebook Page – geni.us/DaleMayerFBFanPage
Facebook Group – geni.us/DaleMayerFBGroup
BookBub – geni.us/DaleMayerBookbub
Instagram – geni.us/DaleMayerInstagram
Goodreads – geni.us/DaleMayerGoodreads
Newsletter – geni.us/DaleNews

Also by Dale Mayer

Published Adult Books:

Hathaway House
Aaron, Book 1
Brock, Book 2
Cole, Book 3
Denton, Book 4
Elliot, Book 5
Finn, Book 6
Gregory, Book 7
Heath, Book 8
Iain, Book 9
Jaden, Book 10
Keith, Book 11

The K9 Files
Ethan, Book 1
Pierce, Book 2
Zane, Book 3
Blaze, Book 4
Lucas, Book 5
Parker, Book 6
Carter, Book 7
Weston, Book 8

Lovely Lethal Gardens

Arsenic in the Azaleas, Book 1
Bones in the Begonias, Book 2
Corpse in the Carnations, Book 3
Daggers in the Dahlias, Book 4
Evidence in the Echinacea, Book 5
Footprints in the Ferns, Book 6
Gun in the Gardenias, Book 7
Handcuffs in the Heather, Book 8
Ice Pick in the Ivy, Book 9

Psychic Vision Series

Tuesday's Child
Hide 'n Go Seek
Maddy's Floor
Garden of Sorrow
Knock Knock…
Rare Find
Eyes to the Soul
Now You See Her
Shattered
Into the Abyss
Seeds of Malice
Eye of the Falcon
Itsy-Bitsy Spider
Unmasked
Deep Beneath
From the Ashes
Stroke of Death
Psychic Visions Books 1–3

Psychic Visions Books 4–6
Psychic Visions Books 7–9

By Death Series
Touched by Death
Haunted by Death
Chilled by Death
By Death Books 1–3

Broken Protocols – Romantic Comedy Series
Cat's Meow
Cat's Pajamas
Cat's Cradle
Cat's Claus
Broken Protocols 1-4

Broken and... Mending
Skin
Scars
Scales (of Justice)
Broken but... Mending 1-3

Glory
Genesis
Tori
Celeste
Glory Trilogy

Biker Blues
Morgan: Biker Blues, Volume 1
Cash: Biker Blues, Volume 2

SEALs of Honor

Mason: SEALs of Honor, Book 1

Hawk: SEALs of Honor, Book 2

Dane: SEALs of Honor, Book 3

Swede: SEALs of Honor, Book 4

Shadow: SEALs of Honor, Book 5

Cooper: SEALs of Honor, Book 6

Markus: SEALs of Honor, Book 7

Evan: SEALs of Honor, Book 8

Mason's Wish: SEALs of Honor, Book 9

Chase: SEALs of Honor, Book 10

Brett: SEALs of Honor, Book 11

Devlin: SEALs of Honor, Book 12

Easton: SEALs of Honor, Book 13

Ryder: SEALs of Honor, Book 14

Macklin: SEALs of Honor, Book 15

Corey: SEALs of Honor, Book 16

Warrick: SEALs of Honor, Book 17

Tanner: SEALs of Honor, Book 18

Jackson: SEALs of Honor, Book 19

Kanen: SEALs of Honor, Book 20

Nelson: SEALs of Honor, Book 21

Taylor: SEALs of Honor, Book 22

Colton: SEALs of Honor, Book 23

Troy: SEALs of Honor, Book 24

SEALs of Honor, Books 1–3

SEALs of Honor, Books 4–6

SEALs of Honor, Books 7–10

SEALs of Honor, Books 11–13

SEALs of Honor, Books 14–16

SEALs of Honor, Books 17–19

Heroes for Hire

Levi's Legend: Heroes for Hire, Book 1

Stone's Surrender: Heroes for Hire, Book 2

Merk's Mistake: Heroes for Hire, Book 3

Rhodes's Reward: Heroes for Hire, Book 4

Flynn's Firecracker: Heroes for Hire, Book 5

Logan's Light: Heroes for Hire, Book 6

Harrison's Heart: Heroes for Hire, Book 7

Saul's Sweetheart: Heroes for Hire, Book 8

Dakota's Delight: Heroes for Hire, Book 9

Michael's Mercy (Part of Sleeper SEAL Series)

Tyson's Treasure: Heroes for Hire, Book 10

Jace's Jewel: Heroes for Hire, Book 11

Rory's Rose: Heroes for Hire, Book 12

Brandon's Bliss: Heroes for Hire, Book 13

Liam's Lily: Heroes for Hire, Book 14

North's Nikki: Heroes for Hire, Book 15

Anders's Angel: Heroes for Hire, Book 16

Reyes's Raina: Heroes for Hire, Book 17

Dezi's Diamond: Heroes for Hire, Book 18

Vince's Vixen: Heroes for Hire, Book 19

Ice's Icing: Heroes for Hire, Book 20

Johan's Joy: Heroes for Hire, Book 21

Heroes for Hire, Books 1–3

Heroes for Hire, Books 4–6

Heroes for Hire, Books 7–9

Heroes for Hire, Books 10–12

Heroes for Hire, Books 13–15

SEALs of Steel
Badger: SEALs of Steel, Book 1
Erick: SEALs of Steel, Book 2
Cade: SEALs of Steel, Book 3
Talon: SEALs of Steel, Book 4
Laszlo: SEALs of Steel, Book 5
Geir: SEALs of Steel, Book 6
Jager: SEALs of Steel, Book 7
The Final Reveal: SEALs of Steel, Book 8
SEALs of Steel, Books 1–4
SEALs of Steel, Books 5–8
SEALs of Steel, Books 1–8

The Mavericks
Kerrick, Book 1
Griffin, Book 2
Jax, Book 3
Beau, Book 4
Asher, Book 5
Ryker, Book 6
Miles, Book 7
Nico, Book 8
Keane, Book 9
Lennox, Book 10
Gavin, Book 11
Shane, Book 12

Bullard's Battle Series
Ryland's Reach, Book 1

Cain's Cross, Book 2
Eton's Escape, Book 3
Garret's Gambit, Book 4
Kano's Keep, Book 5
Fallon's Flaw, Book 6
Quinn's Quest, Book 7
Bullard's Beauty, Book 8

Collections
Dare to Be You…
Dare to Love…
Dare to be Strong…
RomanceX3

Standalone Novellas
It's a Dog's Life
Riana's Revenge
Second Chances

Published Young Adult Books:

Family Blood Ties Series
Vampire in Denial
Vampire in Distress
Vampire in Design
Vampire in Deceit
Vampire in Defiance
Vampire in Conflict
Vampire in Chaos
Vampire in Crisis
Vampire in Control

Vampire in Charge

Family Blood Ties Set 1–3

Family Blood Ties Set 1–5

Family Blood Ties Set 4–6

Family Blood Ties Set 7–9

Sian's Solution, A Family Blood Ties Series Prequel Novelette

Design series

Dangerous Designs

Deadly Designs

Darkest Designs

Design Series Trilogy

Standalone

In Cassie's Corner

Gem Stone (a Gemma Stone Mystery)

Time Thieves

Published Non-Fiction Books:

Career Essentials

Career Essentials: The Résumé

Career Essentials: The Cover Letter

Career Essentials: The Interview

Career Essentials: 3 in 1

www.ingramcontent.com/pod-product-compliance
Lightning Source LLC
Chambersburg PA
CBHW071535100726